DEITIES AND DEMONS

Comprising
CYTHEREA
and
WITH TOWERS AND TURRETS, CROWNED

I0557996

Charles J. Schneider

DEITIES AND DEMONS

DOUBLE DRAGON

CYTHEREA

*

If it be thus to dream,
still let me sleep!
William Shakespeare
Twelfth Night

Chapter 1
Insomnia

She was a goddess in every sense of the word.
Before her, I was utterly oblivious to the person
within; and after, her divine intervention unveiled
the truth behind my soul's ancient conception.
Under the surface of my physical form, and hiding
behind the name inscribed on my birth certificate,
passport, and driver's license, slept a quiet and
dormant secret that abruptly awoke on that day of
unexpected revelation, when she and I finally met.

Adonis James Broussard: born in 1975, in the
French quarter of New Orleans. I was the son of a
Parisian father and a Greek mother, the only child
born from the union of his mind and her body, his
intellect and her beauty, and his logic and her
intuition. My French father, displaced from Europe
to the States by the circumstances of his academic
career, devoted his life to his scholarly calling, *and*
to my mother. She was his cherished Aegean
beauty: a modern day Helen of Troy with a
Mediterranean sensuality that Aphrodite would have
envied. After her untimely death, my father's life

lost meaning; and not long after, he heard her whisper softly in his ear. Heeding her call, he said his peaceful goodbyes and made his final journey to the other side to meet her.

My father was a Classics professor at Tulane and had high hopes for me: his only son. From a young age, the rich academia that he fostered permeated my day-to-day life. It was my father's love for mythology that spawned my own interest in a similar scholarly concentration; and, following in his footsteps when I pursued my own doctorate, I became a respected authority in ancient cultures by the time I earned my tenured professorship at Yale. My own given name, taken from the Greek legend that was dear to my own father's heart, seemed uncannily (or, rather, embarrassingly) appropriate to my specialty; so I swept *Adonis* under the rug, and became James-or Jamie-to all of my friends and colleagues.

Like my father, I dedicated my life to the field; but unlike him, I never found the woman who could be my own life's goddess. Yes, there were women, but none of them touched my spirit like my mother had moved my father. They loved my body, my face, my name, my titles, and my success with a superficial attraction that never went deeper than the facade of my mortal exterior. What I searched and longed for was a woman who could truly understand the true *Adonis* that slept beneath the blanket of my human covering.

And so, my story begins on a chilly day in early March, right before a birthday that I viewed as a particularly unwelcome milestone in my bachelor's life. I sat, sulking, in my office at the Peabody

6

Museum, sipping my coffee while I graded papers from my Undergraduate seminar on *Myths and Modern Culture*. I had just penned a somewhat biting comment on the second to last paper in the queue-a particularly mediocre effort, which I leniently decided to give a 'C+'-hoping with a yawn that the last one would be better.

The Cypriot Identity Crisis: Ancient Greek and Turkish Influences on Modern Day Cyprus, the title read. "What have we here?" I thought. The topic intrigued me, since my mother was born on the Greek side of this Mediterranean island, living in Paphos until she moved to Paris at age 18, where she later met my father. The student's essay was well written and meticulously researched; and as I scribbled an 'A' on the title page, I flipped back for a moment to his references, curious about the essay's sources.

Gianelli, Korphu, Christianson, Brantford: all of these researchers were familiar names in elite anthropology circles; and while some of them were only acquaintances, most of them were friends, and many of them were direct or indirect collaborators on my own academic projects and grants. *Tealmann, Broadman, Zorcra*-all three of them were prominent leaders in the field... but *Sagapo*? Who in the world was Cytherea Sagapo? I didn't know her; had never even *heard* of her. The student who had written the last essay had cited Sagapo's treatise on the Cypriote myth of Aphrodite and Adonis extensively in his essay, and from what I could tell, the unknown author's commentary on the legend's impact on the modern cultural concept of love seemed insightful and precise.

I wouldn't be satisfied, now, until I had read the complete *Sagapo* thesis. An hour later, I sat in Sterling Memorial Library, thumbing through a 100-page volume that had been published a few years ago by a small Greek publishing house. The piece was entitled *Female Love and Beauty in a Masculine Society: the Myth of Aphrodite and Adonis*, by Cytherea V. Sagapo; and I was impressed, to say the least.

Who was she? Now I simply *had* to know. Since the back cover of the book provided no information at all about her, I would have to do some literary detective work to find out more about the mysterious author who wrote like the world's authority on a topic that was quite dear to my heart. My first call, to Yale Press, rewarded me with the names of some contacts at Cronos Publishers; and a few days later, after several back and forth emails, I had what I needed. I wrote Ms. Sagapo an electronic message that night, and her response was pleasant, friendly-and, to my surprise, immediate.

You are very kind, Professor, she said in her email. *I wrote that book many years ago, when I attended University in Athens. I live in Paphos now, where I teach school. My students are eager to learn about our heritage and legends, but I am afraid that most of them are not able to appreciate the written result of my college studies. You see, they are only ten and eleven year olds!*

Such a talent, wasted in a small town elementary school! *I apologize in advance if my comments seem overly intrusive,* I responded after we had switched to instant messaging, *but you could have had a brilliant career if you had pursued an academic path. Did you ever consider attending graduate school?*

I am happy here, Professor-for the most part. Our messages, fueled by the miracle of modern electronic communication, raced back and forth across an ocean and a sea with instantaneous speed. *My students keep me sharp, and I do so love this place, where I was born and raised.*

It's never too late. I ventured a bit further, just slightly over the edge and into the realm of her personal space. *May I ask your age, Ms. Sagapo?*

You certainly may, Professor. I am 27 years old. And you should call me Cytherea, please!

At 27, she was 13 years younger than I was-the exact difference in age between my mother and my father! Could it simply be coincidence? *I don't think you recognize your own talent* (or the connection between the two of us that felt stronger, to me, than the pull of gravity). *You are a very young woman, and should pursue your doctorate. I have friends in Athens; or, you could come here. I would gladly take you under my wing at Yale.*

What was I saying? I didn't know the first thing about her-GPA, academic standing in college, or even the most basic of her academic credentials... except, of course, that she had written a one hundred page anthropological treatment of the Aphrodite myth when she had been an undergraduate that could have easily passed for a PhD thesis! I told myself to trust my instincts. She was worth it. Somehow, I simply *knew* that she was worth it." *And you should call me Jamie,* I added. *It's what all of my friends call me.* I wanted desperately for her to be my friend... and more.

She didn't respond; and, with a sinking heart, I stared at my eerily quiet computer screen until the early morning hours, when I finally fell asleep with my head resting on folded arms at my desk. Had I offended her by complimenting her intellect? Or, had she decided that our conversation had become too friendly-too personal, somehow? Perhaps she had sensed my excitement, backing off as a reaction to my admittedly premature romantic aspirations. These thoughts, and others, plagued my fitful two hours of sleep. Did she have dark hair, or light? Were her eyes a smoky brown, a smoldering green, or blue like the Aegean Sea? Was she slim, or voluptuous? Was she married, divorced, or single? Was she in a relationship, or were there still moist remnants of tears on her perfect alabaster cheeks from a recently ended love affair? Who was she, really? I found myself imagining that she was my own soul's goddess, just as my mother had been to my father-a crazy midnight intuition that sunrise eventually transformed into conviction.

The next day, I taught my courses in a sleep-deprived fog; and that evening, I sat at a corner table in the back, immediately adjacent to the small bar and facing the dark and quiet stage (since there were never any musical acts performing on Mondays) at my favorite club, with my old friend Reginald Winks-a Jurisprudence Professor of *Contracts* and *Torts* at the Law School, who also had a small legal practice on the side. We had known each other forever it seemed, first meeting at our Undergraduate school orientation on the sprawling lawn of Yale's central quad over twenty years ago. Born in London and educated at Eaton, he had married the girl that he started dating our freshman year; and as a result, he had only returned once to his native England to pack up some belongings and relocate permanently to New Haven.

"It looks like you haven't slept in days, Jamie," he commented in his slightly Americanized English accent, as he motioned for the waiter to refill his drink.

"I only slept two hours last night. It's the strangest thing, Reggie. This girl has done something to me, and I know close to nothing about her."

"Has she published anything else?"

"Not a thing. She wrote that book her last year at college in Athens, on her own as far as I can tell, with no co-authors or sponsors."

"Well, it sounds like your professional interest in her is justified. But the rest... "

"I know. It's absolutely ludicrous, but I just have to meet her, Reggie. This verges on obsession."

"Verges? It sounds to me like it *is* an obsession." He shrugged. "I guess you could go there-meet with her on the pretext of a recruitment interview or something. Do you think she might be interested in attending graduate school here?"

"I don't know. I suggested that, but she hasn't answered. It's been a whole day, and her silence is killing me."

"Well, there *is* the time difference. I'm willing to wager you'll find a message from her when you get home tonight."

"I hope so." I took another sip of my Glenlivet. "The coincidences are uncanny, really. She's

Greek-from Paphos, just like my mother; and the 13 year age difference between us is exactly the same as it was between my parents. And finally, there's the literary connection."

"You mean Adonis and Cytherea?"

"Of course. Cytherea is a synonym for Aphrodite; and my father, God rest his soul, found some scholarly amusement in naming me after his favorite mythological character." I paused for a moment, just for effect. "Don't you think it's odd," I continued, "that the 'goddess of love' would write a thesis that has been lost in obscurity, exploring the relationship between the two most famous lovers in Greek mythology and the impact of that ancient fable on modern romance?"

He shook his head. "I think you're manipulating the data to fit your dreamer's theory. You know what this is all about, don't you?"

"Of course I do. She's my destiny." I realized from the look he gave me that he thought I was off my rocker, but by now I didn't care. "Her middle initial is 'V'. I haven't asked her yet, but I'd be willing to bet the house that it stands for Venus."

"Slow down, Jamie. All of this is part of a mid-life crisis. Next week your life's clock turns over into the next decade-a milestone that has apparently pushed you over the edge. It's time you faced your own mortality, my friend. No one lives forever; not even a demigod like Adonis, your namesake."

"This is no mid-life crisis. Forty doesn't bother me." Or did it? I found myself studying the empty bottom of my cocktail glass rather than meeting his perceptive gaze because deep down, I knew he was right. I motioned the waiter for a refill. "There's something else, too. Her last name means *I love you.*"

Reggie looked at me quizzically. "In Greek, I assume?"

I nodded as the waiter topped off my glass. "Yes, indeed. S'agapo-*agapo* with the conjunction-means *I love you* in Greek. This all seems to connect, in a strange way. I'm going to book my flight tomorrow, and don't try to talk me out of it."

"But you don't even know what she looks like, or whether she's even available. She could be married, for all you know!"

"If she is, then so be it. I'll be traveling to Paphos to recruit her as a graduate student, remember? If my romantic aspirations don't pan out, it's not the end of the world. At least I'll get a nice vacation out of the deal-and maybe a talented anthropology student, to boot."

It was 12 midnight by the time I got home, which meant it was 7 AM there. "Please message me," I begged out loud; and sure enough, right there on my tablet my wish had materialized.

I have to admit that I do miss the stimulation from those days. I have a few other manuscripts that you might be interested in seeing. They are not complete, though. They need some work, but one of them in particular might work as a graduate thesis. Then, in a second message balloon that the time-caption indicated she had written an hour after the first: *I apologize for being so forward. You are a very busy Professor. I am so sorry to waste your time.*

I answered in a panic. *I have been out. I'm so very happy to hear from you! Of course I'd love to*

13

see your other manuscripts, and would very much like to meet you as well.

Her response was immediate, and so fantastic that I had to rub my eyes and blink a few times to make sure that what I read was real. *I thought it was you. Please come immediately.*

Do we know each other? I typed.

Just come. I know you feel the same.

She was right, I *did* feel it-a certain connection that whispered a happily decisive 'destiny' in my ear. I didn't waste any time logging onto the British Airways website, making my reservation then and there with an uncharacteristic spontaneity that, oddly, made me feel more alive than I had in years. By 1 AM, after I had also booked my hotel and a car rental, I realized that I'd be there for my birthday, and couldn't imagine a better gift to myself. It was all meant to be, it seemed-and incredibly, I'd be leaving first thing in the morning. It didn't take me long to pack; and before I knew it I was tossing and turning in bed, much too excited to sleep.

In just five hours, I would climb into the backseat of the airport limousine that I had just booked on-line; in eight hours, I would embark on my flight to Paphos via London and Athens; and in eighteen hours, I would be settling into my hotel in Greek Cyprus-one step closer to my imagined goddess of love, whose middle initial *did*, incredibly, stand for Venus (*my mother was enamored with our island's patron goddess*, she had explained).

Can I see a picture of you? I asked, bleary eyed with insomnia, my tablet on my lap.

14

We'll meet soon enough, it would ruin the surprise.

Can we talk on the phone?

No. You must be patient. Sleep now.

I can't.

You will. She typed the command, and almost instantly my eyes felt heavy and I couldn't stay awake another moment.

I was out.

Chapter 2
Jet Lag

I deplaned in London, then in Athens, finally arriving at Paphos International Airport after a tiring twelve-hour journey. I had always had difficulty sleeping in coach-class seats, and this trip was no exception. By the time I arrived in Cyprus, I felt severely jet-lagged.

I picked up my rental car, entered the hotel address into the navigator system, and drove directly to my quaint accommodations at the top of a winding cobblestoned hill. As soon as I arrived, checking in completely exhausted and with dreams of the soft feather bed waiting for me upstairs, I took the elevator up to the second floor landing; turned the key in the lock to my room (lucky thirteen); threw my suitcase into the corner; turned down the bed-sheets; and fell immediately into a deep and refreshing sleep.

I awoke to the ring of my phone-the 6 pm wake-up call that I had requested at check-in. Two hours would be plenty of time to ready myself for the 8 PM reservations that she had made for us at *Taverna Hephaestus*, which was located conveniently within walking distance of my hotel. After a shower and shave, I found myself walking down the street, map in hand, on my way to meet my destiny.

Hephaestus was the ancient god of Fire, and Aphrodite's mythological husband. This was, of course, a perfectly logical name for a restaurant in

Cyprus-especially one that specialized in grilled seafood and other flamed delicacies. Still, I found myself pondering the irony of yet another incredible coincidence. How strange that I would soon meet Cytherea-aka Aphrodite-in a restaurant named after the goddess's lame and neglected spouse. He eventually played cuckold to his brother Ares, who wooed Aphrodite and won her over, for a time. My namesake lured her away, of course, with the promise of true love; but the whole affair did not end well, for Adonis at least. I hoped for a better outcome in the here and now, as I rounded the last corner on my walking tour, finally reaching the restaurant well in advance of our reservation time.

The restaurant was dark, quiet, and intimate-a perfect setting for our first meeting. I nervously scanned the small room for signs of my mysterious blind date. The restaurant could accommodate perhaps a dozen small parties at the most, and all of the tables except for one were occupied. I noted with more than slight relief that there were no unaccompanied women on the premises. The perspiration on my forehead was not entirely due to the brisk walk from the hotel to the restaurant, and a few moments alone at our table before she arrived would help to calm my nerves and still my pounding heart.

I was greeted cordially by a tall maître-de with coal black hair. He smiled insincerely, and did not speak. He had undoubtedly judged correctly from my appearance that I was a tourist with an embarrassingly scant Greek vocabulary.

Cytherea had told me that the reservations would be in her name; so clearing my throat, and hoping that my bland American accent would not butcher the correct pronunciation, I made my bold announcement. "Sagapo," I stated with feigned assurance, shoving my hands into my pockets as I watched him look down at his reservation list.

He shook his head. "No," he said, glancing back in my direction and raising his eyebrows suspiciously.

Mildly surprised that she would not use her surname to reserve our table, I offered her given name instead. "Cytherea," I suggested hopefully. He scanned the list with a skeptical expression on his face.

"No," he concluded, shaking his head again for emphasis. "There is no reservation under *either* name, unfortunately," he said.

At least he spoke English, but he was not about to engage in any verbal pleasantries with a mere tourist. He started to turn away, the contempt obvious in his shrug as he began attending to more important matters. His abrupt dismissal made my face burn self-consciously as I glanced longingly at the only empty table, which I knew belonged to us.

I found myself involved in a ludicrous subconscious dialogue with my absent partner. *What would you have me do now, my sweet goddess of love?* Then, it struck me. It seemed so obvious, so simple... and so perfect. "Check under the name *Aphrodite*, please," I suggested, confidant that this time I'd hit pay dirt.

My examiner frowned, obviously disappointed that I had given the correct answer this time. He bowed, contemptuously I thought. "Right this way, sir." He led me to the table for two that I had fought to procure, where I pulled out the nearest chair myself since he didn't make a move to do so himself. I was pleased to discover that my seat afforded me an ideal view of the street and restaurant's entryway through a large picture window. I watched for her arrival expectantly as a handful of couples strolled by arm-in-arm, followed by a group of raucous students and then by an elderly man who was being rather obviously walked by his leashed mastiff rather than vice versa. Thirty minutes passed, during which time I saw no passers-by who would even vaguely fit my imagined vision of the beautiful Aphrodite.

I finished two glasses of native Agiogitiko (highly recommended by my waiter) while I waited for my fantasy; and still, no sign of her. I glanced at my watch nervously, noticing that it was now forty-five minutes past our reservation time. My dejection deepened as more time elapsed. Had she stood me up? Perhaps she had; and if so, I could hardly believe I had been duped so easily. As I sat lamenting my gullible vulnerability, I felt a tap on my shoulder as the maître-de handed me a folded note.

"For you, sir," he stated victoriously as he turned abruptly to go. My heart was in my throat as I noticed that *Jamie* was written on the outside of the letter in a feminine hand. I gently grabbed the maitre-de's elbow, rising from my chair with unsophisticated haste.

"Who gave you this note?" I demanded, waving the unread folded piece of paper under his nose.

He looked at me calmly, intentionally prolonging the torture with an unnecessary pause.

19

"Only the most beautiful woman I have ever seen," he finally responded, apparently pleased that she would not be having dinner with such a contemptible American tourist.

"Where is she?" I asked, looking wildly around the restaurant as if I might spot her standing in a corner or against the wall.

He shrugged. "Gone, just as quickly as she came," he said, pointing behind him towards the restaurant's door. "She left immediately, after handing me the note."

My heart sank; I would never find her now. I had no idea what she looked like, which of course meant that any attempt at pursuit would be truly pointless. Understanding that I could not follow a faceless specter, and also realizing that I had been undone by my own naive romanticism, I sat back down at my corner table. I felt a strange acceptance wash over me as I unfolded the note to quietly read what she had written.

My dear Jamie,

Finding you was no coincidence. I've been searching for many, many years-finally losing hope, until that day when your name appeared so unexpectedly on my computer screen. I knew that it had to be you; and now, we will finally be reunited.

As I stood in the shadows across the street, I watched you arrive and studied your all too familiar profile as you sat at our table by the window. Seeing you again is an answer to my prayers, and all of my doubts have disappeared. Now that I've confirmed that you are really you, we need to celebrate-but the restaurant is much too busy. Please meet me in a more private place.

I'll be waiting for you in 'Old Paphos,' just a few miles from here, at Aphrodite's Temple very near 'Petra tou Romiou': the rock where the goddess herself emerged from the sea in the ancient days. Follow the beach road to the ruins, and use the northeast entrance. I will leave the gate unlocked. And please, darling, make sure you're not seen. For reasons I'll explain later, it's crucial that our meeting remain a secret. I've waited patiently for what seems like an eternity! And now, finally, I'll be able to feel your tender and gentle touch.

Cytherea.

'Reunited'... 'all too familiar profile'... 'confirmed that you are really you'-what in the world was going on here? She wrote as if we knew each other in some sort of mutual past that she recalled, but I didn't. She even referred to me as 'darling'! How did she know me? I wracked my brains, searching my past for any clues about the mysterious Cytherea Sagapo. She couldn't have been a student in any of my classes-unless, of course, she was hiding her real identity behind a fictitious name. Perhaps she wasn't Cytherea at all. Could she be Janet... or Sylvie... or Bridgette? What if a previous lover had assumed this strange Cytherea identity, arranging a romantic reunion in far-off and exotic Cyprus, in order to rekindle an ancient romance?

But she had written the book, after all-that much seemed true; and didn't that validate her existence as Ms. Sagapo? *No, not really.* Cytherea could easily be a pen name, and I could very well be looking into the eyes of some old flame tonight, or

21

even an old colleague, rather than my imagined fantasy lover and would-be academic prodigy.

But, then again, there was that odd connection that I sensed, even from the very first electronic message-and she felt it too, quite obviously, given the strangely personal letter from her that I held in my trembling fingers. Was I delusional? Or, could there really be something magical and unbelievable at work in this strange, blossoming relationship?

Well, there was only one way to find out. I put some money on the table; and turning to leave, I heard the maître-de speaking to an older couple in Greek. Although I couldn't understand the words, it was clear from his gestures that he was turning them away. The couple looked disappointed. Approaching from behind, I kindly touched the gentleman's shoulder.

"You can have my table," I offered, unsure if the older man understood English.

"So unfortunate that your dining partner had other plans," the maître-de said, shaking his head in mock sympathy.

I turned to go, initially intending to ignore him but then changing my mind. "Actually, I'll be meeting her elsewhere," I explained over my shoulder, one foot over the threshold onto the sidewalk. "This place just doesn't meet our high standards." *Touché*.

Chapter 3
Sleepwalking

My navigator, programmed in English, easily found Aphrodite's Temple in its *point of interest* icon; and a few moments later, I was leaving Paphos town center heading into a full moon on a beachside road. The terrain was low and rocky to my right; and on my left, the low tide had opened a broad expanse of sand that slipped underneath the rush of surf, at least one hundred yards beyond. The ruins sat ahead of me on a jagged hillside, the granite blocks haphazardly mixed with the silver marble remains of antiquity's magnificence.

As I pulled up on the side of the road (directly in front of the northeast entryway as she had instructed), I looked up on the hill, noticing rows and rows of intact columns standing like petrified trees on the raised platform of the temple's newly reconstructed foundation. If she meant for us to meet up there, it would take me quite a while to navigate the footpath that I saw winding through the stones and up the hillside, beginning on the other side of a ten-foot high construction fence, much too high to climb over, that guarded the entire perimeter. I would have to gain access to the interior through the gate that she had referenced, which I spotted just to the right along with a sign posted on the crisscross of metal that warned people like me not to trespass.

I shut off the engine, opened the door, and got out. Was she here? I looked around. My car stood alone on the deserted road, so I must have arrived first, but this didn't quite add up. Her note said that she would be waiting for me, but I saw no sign of her anywhere. Could there be an access road, or a parking lot, behind the ruins? I squinted, just making out the shadowy outline of a museum or a tourist center off to the side, concluding with a self-assuring node that she must have parked her car up there. With fresh resolve, I locked the doors with the vehicle's remote and started towards my destination.

True to her word, the gate was unlocked. A moment later I was on the other side, picking my way through crumbling rocks and teetering boulders while I cautiously followed the perilous and winding pathway through the rugged terrain and up the hillside. Obviously, this approach to the Temple, which was in dire need of repair, was little used. The surroundings, and the atmosphere, felt surreal; and if someone had later told me that I had been sleepwalking in some kind of bizarre dream as I headed up that deserted path, I wouldn't have argued otherwise. Nearing the top, I carefully navigated some steps that led to a dangerously narrow resting platform, finally reaching the foundation wall with a sigh of relief... *and* a cry of exasperation.

I stood facing a sheer and smooth granite wall that towered at least fifteen feet upwards: an unclimbable barricade with no visible footholds that would surely prevent my access to the temple from the ground, at least at *this* location. How in the world was I supposed to get up there? Had she really meant for me to enter on this side?

And then I saw it: a faint brush of whiteness on the grey palette of the building's edge. Approaching closer, I saw a hemp ladder dangling over the edge from above, swaying gently in the warm ocean breeze. I smiled, testing the ladder's stability with two brisk tugs. Feeling satisfied that it had been adequately secured at the top, I climbed quickly up and over onto the foundation's platform.

I looked around. The vestige of a supporting wall interrupted an interior line of columns; and further ahead, yet another internal rectangle of columns surrounded a raised stone platform: the altar itself. The place was eerily deserted. *Where is she?* I wondered, making my way carefully around this pile and that pile of rock and stone debris towards Aphrodite's central ritual site. I could see well enough because the roofless structure offered no obstruction for the moonlight, which shone brightly onto the surviving columns and blocks of stone to cast inky Rorschach-like shadows onto the granite floor. The shadow to my left looked like the silhouette of Diana with her bow, and the shadow to my right could be easily dreamed into Apollo with his harp. I shivered involuntarily by the time I had reached the ritual altar, a little bit unnerved by my imaginings as well as the surroundings.

Why would she want to meet me here, of all places? It was private, yes; but as I looked skeptically around, I quickly became convinced that the corner table at *Taverna Hephaestus* would have been a far better location to make our initial acquaintance than these deserted ruins. On the other hand, Aphrodite's Temple had definite romantic appeal-appropriate, perhaps, for my first 'face-to-face' encounter with my own personal goddess of love? I sat down on the altar. "I'm here, Aphrodite," I said out loud, tongue partly in cheek.

I was startled to hear a response. "And I'm here too, Adonis."

I jumped up in surprise and took a few steps back, truly unsure if the vision was conjured or real; but there she was, truly the most beautiful woman that I had ever seen, wearing a toga and reclining right there on the stone altar, not even three feet away from me, appearing abruptly and literally out of thin air, in a spot that a few seconds earlier had definitely been quite unoccupied. Was she flesh and blood, delusional fantasy, or something supernatural? Her walnut-colored hair shimmered in the moonlight; and her eyes (a dark and rich hazel containing flecks of emerald) gazed back at me with an amused twinkle.

"Who... what... " I cleared my throat in embarrassment. This woman *couldn't* be Cytherea. "I was supposed to meet someone here-a schoolteacher."

"I know; and here I am!"

I cocked my head, quizzically. "Ms. Sagapo?"

She waved her hand dismissively. "The last name is fabricated-it means *I love you* in Greek, you know; but I'm Cytherea all right. I use that particular first name because the reference to 'goddess of love' is a bit more obscure than my other ones."

"Which would be... ?"

Even though I expected her answer, which of course didn't clarify her real identity one bit, I couldn't help but feel like a psychiatric patient whose doctor had just signed off on the hospital discharge papers because his delusions had just been verified as reality. "Aphrodite is my preferred name; but in some circles I'm know as Venus, too."

"So what should *I* call you?"

"Aphrodite, if you please. It's my favorite."

Now things were *really* getting strange, if she actually expected me to call her Aphrodite. I stepped closer and sat back down on the edge of the sacrificial alter. "You took me a little bit by surprise. You see, just a minute ago you weren't here; and now you are... somehow... " My voice trailed off, as I scratched my head and tried to rationalize her abrupt arrival. Could I have overlooked her lying there in the shadows? That seemed unlikely, since I had been sitting right next to her when she had magically materialized.

"I won't bite," she laughed, patting the stone next to her with an open palm. "Come over here a little bit closer, Adonis. We have a lot of catching up to do, my long-lost love."

I pulled my legs up onto the raised slab of stone and scooted over, close enough so that she was able to touch my hand. Her skin felt smooth and warm, and the contact sent shivers up my spine. "You see," she whispered, "I'm real."

It was too good to be true in the 'certifiably crazy' sense of the phrase. "Who are you-*really*?" I asked gently.

"Well, let's just say that I'm *exactly* who you dreamed I'd be."

I looked into the depths of her hazel eyes. "I've fantasized about the woman I've been searching for all of my life in so many different ways. If you're

27

'her', then my soul's deepest desire has been answered." It may have sounded overly maudlin, but it was true. She was the perfect epitome of my imagined other-half.

"You've been searching for me, and I've been searching for you. It's been a long time for both of us, Adonis."

"My name *is* actually Adonis, but no one calls me that. I'm Jamie."

"Not to me. You don't understand yet, but you will." She pulled me down, and her kiss was long, soft, deep-and oddly familiar. "My sweet Adonis," she whispered. "I think you should know... "

The abruptness of it all was startling. She broke off her thought in mid-sentence, pulling away from me and looking furtively around, at first towards the side of the temple facing the ocean, and then up to the heavens. Her eyes betrayed a quickly escalating sense of panic.

"What is it, Aphrodite?" If she wanted me to call her that, I would. Why not? A little role-playing never hurt a blossoming romance, if past experience held true.

"What have I done?" she said in horror, her voice low.

I gazed at her skeptically. "What is it, exactly, that you think you've done?"

"Only ruined everything, potentially. I thought we'd be safe here; and we *would* have been, if only I hadn't kissed you and whispered your name. I couldn't help myself, though. It's been so long, Adonis."

I was starting to think that she really *did* suffer from some kind of mental illness-paranoid

28

schizophrenia, perhaps? "Do you think we've been discovered?" I followed her gaze towards the water, and then up to the sky. "I don't see anyone." Had she heard an approaching security guard? I wondered how an American tourist would fare in a Greek prison as I pictured the both of us in handcuffs, being led away sheepishly by a stern and humorless policeman for trespassing on government property. What an embarrassing way *that* would be, to end our first date.

She was wringing her hands in distress. "I should have been more careful. He felt my emotions surge when we kissed, which was bad enough; but then he heard me think and speak your name."

"In God's name, who are you talking about?"

"Not 'God', but *a* god: Ares. We have to hide you, Adonis, right away." She looked around frantically for an appropriate place. "I'll have to use my magic... "

"This has *got* to be some sort of joke." I stood up, insulted. "I'm not an idiot, you know!"

She stared me down with a sternness that screamed 'I'm serious' in the face of what was clearly ludicrous. "This is no joke. If he discovers you here, he'll kill you! I have to hide you immediately; there's no time to lose!"

"I'm gullible, but I can recognize a practical joke when I see one. I think I'll be going now, 'Aphrodite'."

Her eyes burned with anger, dousing my sarcasm instantaneously. "Don't say my name, he's sure to hear it and sense you too. You don't understand. You're in grave danger, and he'll be here in a matter of seconds. Now that I've finally

29

found you again, I will *not* let him kill you like he did before!" She took my face in her hands to lock our gazes. "There's no time! Look into my eyes, ancient lover, and suspend your disbelief. Relax your will, and let me transform you."

If she spoke the truth, my life was at stake; so I nodded my agreement, as I quickly lost myself in her intoxicating eyes. I felt her touch me, deep inside. "You can have me-heart and soul," I said, mesmerized, as I felt her literally permeate me with some kind of strange telepathic essence. She was in control now, and I couldn't even *dream* of resisting her.

A split second later, I felt a searing pain behind my eyes; but then it was over. I tried to move, but my limbs felt heavy and thick. Was I paralyzed? As my vision came slowly into focus, I saw her standing alone next to the temple's altar.

I couldn't turn my head-it was simply too dense, too solid, and definitely too stationary. I felt like... a piece of stone.

And then-suddenly-I knew what she had done. I felt like a stone, because I *was* a stone! Incredibly, impossibly, and unbelievably, Aphrodite had turned me into a marble pillar.

Chapter 4
Sleep Paralysis

Stay perfectly still, her subconsciously-projected voice whispered in my ear. *If you try to stir, he'll sense you in the stone; and if he finds you, he'll make the transformation permanent. Try not to move, and I'll distract him with some harmless seduction.*

Despite the seriousness of my predicament, I had to laugh. Just a few minutes earlier, I had just kissed the most beautiful woman I'd ever seen, and now I was being held captive (granted, for my own safety, but still imprisoned, nonetheless) within a crumbling rock pillar.

I had to face the facts, now, since they were staring me right in the face. She was Aphrodite, I guess-the real deal; although some other possibilities quickly came to mind. Was I lying passed out under the table at *Taverna Hephaestus*, having been drugged by the jealous and vindictive maître-de? Or more plausibly, could I actually be fast asleep in my bed at home in New Haven having the craziest dream of my life? True or imagined, here I was; and I found myself, despite my dwindling but still potent skepticism, concentrating on relaxing my limbs. Why? Because the mirage named Aphrodite insisted that I was in grave danger.

Just stay still, she commanded sternly. *Your life depends on it!*

31

I'm trying! Get rid of him quickly, please, before rigor mortis sets in. My half-hearted attempt at humor seemed to fall on deaf ears, since she was intensely focused on the empty air directly in front of her, apparently expecting a visitor who would require her full attention. I found myself wondering what sort of relationship Aphrodite had with Ares now, after their humiliating break-up. I knew all the myths, of course, and the story of Ares and Aphrodite was one of the spiciest ones involving love, seduction, promiscuity, and infidelity. Aphrodite, who was married to Hephaestus at the time, had three children with Ares while they were lovers. When Hephaestus discovered Ares in bed with his wife one day, he captured the amorous couple in a net, and then summoned all of the gods to gather around them in order to expose and ridicule the powerful god of war. Although the story ends there, the general consensus (in scholarly and popular circles) is that the public discovery of their affair put a permanent end to their relationship. I decided 'what the hell', and just came right out and asked her-telepathically, of course. *So what's the deal now between you and Ares?*

Well, our souls are still connected-an unfortunate consequence of our romantic history. He never really got over me, and I'm embarrassed to say that he still keeps very close tabs on me. It's infuriating, really. I'm an obsession, and nothing I say or do has any effect, whatsoever, on his persistence.

A surge of insecurity swept over me like a tidal wave. Could she possibly have feelings for him, still? I couldn't help but wonder that if I was lucky enough to *physically* survived the next ten or fifteen minutes, would Ares ultimately prove to be the author of my emotional devastation instead? Now that I had found her, how could I possibly live without my beautiful Aphrodite?

Quiet now, Adonis. Here he is.

In the empty air directly in front of her, there now stood a man-muscular, handsome, and dressed only in a loincloth; and then, with a start, I realized that I had seen him before. *He killed me!* A horrifying vision of Ares, disguised as a boar, flashed in my mind's eye, his tusks stained and dripping with *my* blood. The myth, it seemed, was more than a simple fable, and I had actually *lived* it. Could this possibly be happening to me? Could I actually be the *real* Adonis?

The story of Adonis' death (correction, *my* death) suddenly took on a more personal meaning. A handful of mythological scholars speculate that Persephone, who had romantic 'custody' of Adonis for a third of each year, sent the boar to kill Adonis to spite Aphrodite (who enjoyed Adonis as a 'live-in' lover for the remaining two-thirds), while a few others insist that Artemis was behind the attack because she was jealous of Adonis' hunting skills; but the vast majority of sources contend that the boar was actually a shape-shifted Ares, who was out for revenge because Aphrodite's affections had focused away from him and onto Adonis. Now I knew that the majority opinion was the correct one, because in my newly refreshed memory I witnessed Ares (the same man who now stood just a few paces away from me in this bizarre 'I can see you but you can't see me' arrangement) morph into the deadly beast and impale me on his razor-sharp tusks. I shivered with the clarity of the recollection, but quickly pulled myself out of the past and into the present when I realized that Aphrodite and Ares were engaged in a heated discussion.

"I'm getting tired of this, Ares," she was saying. "I should be able to live my life without having you constantly chaperone my every move. This borders on harassment."

"You know what Zeus ruled, honey. It was all detailed in the court transcript, and spelled out in the judge's order. Do I have to remind you that the reincarnation of Adonis, *wherever* he is, will die if you're intimate with another man? I'm just trying to protect him by helping you lower the thermometer on your over-heated libido."

"You must think I'm an idiot. I'm perfectly aware of the ruling, Ares; but *my* question to *you* is this: why do you care if that happens? If I sleep with someone else, Adonis will be out of the picture. Isn't that what you've always wanted, anyway? Really, Ares, you're behaving a lot like a mentally crazed stalker."

He smiled. "I'd love to see Adonis pushing up daisies; but that's just the thing! I want to *see* him die-actually *witness* the scene, rather than just imagining the peaceful disintegration of his physical body that would occur if you slept with someone other than him."

"So, you're hoping to catch me before I do the 'nasty' with some muscle-ripped stud, and prevent it so you can have the opportunity to kill Adonis yourself?"

"Bingo. But just between you and me, I have a dual agenda." He paused, waiting for her to react, but she just stood there, as silent as the pillar I was trapped in. "Don't you want to hear?" he finally asked.

"Is it any different than all of your previous explanations?" She stood impatiently now with her arms crossed, tapping one foot and rolling her eyes. Her entire demeanor said 'let's just get this over with', but Ares seemed oblivious to her lack of engagement. He was just that kind of guy, I seemed to recall.

"Well, think about it. Every time I sense a romantic emotion coming from you, I can't help but suspect that you've finally located him, after all of these long centuries. And if I can catch you with *Adonis*... " He grinned sadistically. "Well, let's just say that I'd get immense pleasure from sinking the knife into his stinking gut myself."

"You're sick."

"Of *course* I am. Being the god of violence, war and bloodshed, you can't say it's totally out of character for me to crave this kind of thing, now can you?"

"But this goes way beyond your usual conquer and defeat mentality, Ares. You and I were never married. This long-lasting jealousy needs to end."

"Why? I thrive on the thrill of the hunt; and someday, after I catch Adonis and finish him off, I'll win you back. Most women just *melt* when I kill for them."

"Not me. Been there, done that-remember? You killed Adonis for me once, Ares, and here we are.

35

Quite frankly, your behavior now is severely counterproductive."

"How so?"

"Can't you see that you're pushing me away? I'd be willing to bet you want just the opposite."

He cocked his head. "Does this mean you still have feelings for me?"

"Of course I still have feelings for you," she answered evasively, while giving my column a sidelong glance. "Why wouldn't I?"

He hesitated a moment as he digested her comment, and then held her firmly by both shoulders in order to force her to gaze back at him. "Look me in the eyes, Aphrodite, and tell me that you aren't hiding someone here. I haven't sensed such strong emotional pulsations coming from you for centuries. Is it Adonis? If you were with him here a few moments ago, you won't be able to hide him from me forever." He looked around. "He couldn't have gone far."

"Ares, I *swear* it wasn't him." She moved closer to him, so that their bodies made contact-an extreme measure, I sensed, that she deemed necessary to throw him off my scent. "In fact, there was *no one* here with me. I intentionally willed that emotional surge to call *you*."

"Why would you do that?" His voice wavered slightly, and I sensed his suspicion would shortly lose the battle to the strong-arm of his over-pumped ego. What she said next struck the winning blow.

"Because I want you back, silly."

He blinked twice. "You... what?"

"You heard me. I want you back." She pushed her body a little bit more firmly against his, and the effect was immediate. Before I could blink (which I couldn't because my eyes were glued open with cement), his lips were pressed on hers and his hands were groping her breasts and buttocks. She convincingly reciprocated, touching him in all the right places (to my horrified dismay), but all the while looking towards me to send a very clear message in her eyes. *I'm just appeasing him, Adonis. This means absolutely nothing to me.* I gritted my teeth and tried not to look, but a pillar can't turn its head so I was forced to watch the unfolding spectacle.

Next he predictably undressed her, undoing the clasp on her shoulder so that the toga easily slid off her perfect alabaster nudity, giving me an eye-full of pure heaven while he backed her up against the altar, at least until the broadness of his posterior torso blocked my view. How far would she go? "No," she declared (thank God), pushing him forcefully away and gathering up her gown to cover up her breath-taking naked curves.

"What's your game, woman?" he boomed.

The rage I heard in his voice would make a Minotaur shake with fear, but not Aphrodite. She calmly re-fastened her toga, stepped forward, and put both hands on his chest, silencing him in an instant with her lips, once again, on his. "Not now; not here," I heard her say between kisses. "This is happening so fast. I just need a few days to sort out my feelings, Ares-to say my private goodbyes to Adonis." Ares crinkled his forehead, either in bewilderment or disgust, I couldn't tell which. "You know as well as I do that Adonis will die the minute we couple," she unnecessarily explained. "I'm ok

37

with that, but *surely* you understand that it's not an easy thing to let go of his memory. I need some time." The hard lines on his face seemed to soften, especially when her hands slipped down from his chest to his stomach, and then further. "Can you give me a few days, big guy? It'll be well worth the wait."

He nodded, closing his eyes in response to her caress. "I understand," he finally said.

"Good," she said, stepping away from him and sitting on the end of the altar. "Patience is a virtue, lover; and I promise you a *very* lusty pay-off."

"We need to take this to the next level soon, though." Was that actually a *pout* on his face? This guy was unbelievable-more like a randy teenager, or a kid that never grew up, rather than one of the most powerful gods in the line-up of major Greek deities. He sat next to her on the altar with his arms crossed. "Explain something to me."

"Anything."

"Why have you given up on Adonis all of a sudden? I thought he was your 'one and only'."

"Think about it, Ares. I've been searching for him all these years, with nothing at all to show for it. I've come to realize that I'll *never* find him, and why waste any more of my time on such an impossible task? I'm just tired; and, after so much time, my feelings for him have cooled down anyway. Even if I *did* find him, I'm not sure it would be the same between us."

Ares nodded. "That makes perfect sense. Why keep searching for the love of your life when he's sitting right in front of you? Finally, you've seen the light!" His pretentious grin couldn't help but infuriate me, but what could I do? Even if I wasn't mortared into a stone pillar, I would be no match for the massive and powerful god of war.

"Exactly. I've had more than enough time to think about things, Ares. I want *you*, and no one else." She sounded so convincing. I hoped to God it was a lie.

"Good choice, Aphrodite. After all, I *am* the best!"

I felt my blood boiling. If I had been able to materialize out of the rock, I would have, despite the danger. One carefully placed kick would be enough to readjust his arrogance, I thought, imagining with relish the impact of shoe-on-loincloth that would cause him to drop to his knees, incapacitated by the visceral pain in his crotch.

"Yes, I remember." She had her hand on his arm, squeezing his biceps while she simultaneously stroked his ridiculously-inflated ego with her well-chosen words. "This brings us to the final reason I'm willing to let Adonis go. Let's face it, Ares; I've been celibate for much, *much* too long. I need it. More specifically, I need *you*."

He moved a little bit closer, fiddling with her toga clasp. "So tell me again-why can't we copulate now?" I shook my head internally. He was as romantic as a randy gorilla.

She gently took his hand off the gown and held it between her two palms. "Try to put your hormones away for a minute, Ares. This is a big, big step for me-*huge*, in fact. Once you and I are intimate, Adonis will disappear... *forever*. That's not something that I can take lightly. Just give me a few days to put my feelings for him away."

"Alright, I'll give you some time." His expression turned suddenly from pliable to menacing. "But, by Zeus, if you're toying with me Aphrodite, my anger has no limits."

"I know all about your temper, Ares. I love you-I always have."

She played the charade like an expert, and once again he was the eager puppy rather than the snarling wolf. "I love you, too." He was like putty in her hands. "So should we meet somewhere tomorrow?"

"That's too soon. Let's say at *Demeter's,* in the cottage banquet room where we had the last Olympian board meeting... in three days. Does that suit you?"

"That suits me fine, baby."

Ares sat there stupidly, lingering in the awkward silence as the socially-inept often do. "I'm tired, Ares," she finally declared.

"Not me." He didn't take the hint. Instead, he flexed his pecs and actually inspected them one-by-one with the stereotypical self-absorption of a fanatical body-builder. "Got to hit the gym," he commented, half to himself.

"Well, now would be a good time."

"So we're done, then?" Really? This guy was the poster child for clueless.

"Yes, we're done."

"Can I have another kiss before I go?"

"No, you can't."

"Just a little one?"

She gave him a look that said: 'you have *got* to be kidding;' stood up, and crossed her arms defiantly. "Don't make me call Hera and file a grievance with the GASHAC."

GASHAC? I thought.

'Goddesses Against Sexual Harassment Advocacy Committee,' she explained to me telepathically.

"Okay, okay. No reason to get all 'radical' on me. I get it. Ciao." And with an overstated wink, Ares was finally gone.

Aphrodite rolled her eyes. "He doesn't have a drop of Italian ancestry in him; but still, it's always *ciao* instead of *adio*. I can't believe I fell for that pumped up pretentious jerk, way back when." She walked directly over to my column and started a one-way conversation with it. Anyone looking on would have thought she was totally off her rocker. "His muscle-bound assertiveness used to appeal to me, when I was young and impressionable, but the centuries have changed me. I can't even recognize the woman I used to be. You were, and *are*, such a breath of fresh air. I've never loved anyone like I love you, Adonis."

She spoke now in my head. *Never doubt my love for you, darling. I hope you know that all of this was just an act. I thought for sure he would find you; but now, he's off your scent and onto mine, thank the heavens. He's such a pushover. All it takes is a tiny whiff of feminine pheromone and he's easily 'handled'.*

All I wanted to do was take her in my arms, pledging my life and my love to her for the rest of eternity; but of course I couldn't because my limbs were as mobile as two-ton rocks. *Can we discuss this further with me out there instead of in here?*

41

I'll release you in a minute, when I'm sure it's safe. She looked furtively over her shoulder. *He needs to be far away; and even then, it might be very dangerous for us to stay here together.*

We should go back to the restaurant then. I could really use a drink-or two, or three. Had I actually just propositioned the *real* Aphrodite, asking her to help me wind down over a bottle of Scotch? Funny how something so thoroughly insane could sound perfected sane, but it did. How could it *not*, though, after I had witnessed the more-than-implausible, with my very own eyes. *But if we're going bar-hopping, you'll have to conjure yourself some modern clothes. The ancient toga's okay, but I'm dying to see you in a tight skirt and heels.*

She didn't laugh. *No, that wouldn't be smart.* I could see by her expression that she was weighing our options, and when she announced her conclusion, my heart fell. *We can't be together at all right now.*

You're joking, right?

I'm dead serious. If Ares senses us together, you're done, so we need to stay away from each other tonight.

You mean to tell me that after all this, I can't be with you?

I don't like it any more than you do, but our future together is at stake so we need to play this smart. I won't lose you again now that I've found you, after so many thousands of years.

But I have so many questions!

And they will all be answered in time, but you need to be alive to hear the explanations.

She had a very good point. *Alright, I get it. So what do you propose now, all-knowing and ever-wise one?*

Meet me the day after tomorrow, in Polis: a small town on the northwest coast, where we first met. You'll find nice accommodations at a resort near the monastery of Gialia. I'll leave a message for you at your hotel, confirming our rendezvous time at the Baths of Aphrodite. Do you remember?

I remember. How could I forget? I had been hunting in the Akamas forest and stopped to quench my thirst at a spring-fed pond surrounded by flowers and overlooking the bay. As I stepped from tree-cover, there she was, swimming naked in the crystal-clear water. Our eyes locked and it was love at first sight, for me *and* for her, at that secluded place that legend later christened 'the Baths of Aphrodite'. We had each other for the first time there, beginning partly submerged in the water with her lean thighs gripped tightly around my waist, and then ending on the moss-covered pond-side, our bodies locked together with her on top and then with positions reversed until we had both had our fill. I had never known such passion before then, or after.

Meet me there in two days.

I will. I needed to scratch an itch but I couldn't because my arms had been turned into cinderblocks. *Can you get me out of here, please, before my heart turns to stone like the rest of me?*

She looked behind her and then from side-to-side, confirming that we were still alone. *Yes, I think it's safe now, but there's one more thing. After*

43

I release you, go directly to a nightclub in downtown Paphos. It's called Caduceus.

I'm not really in the mood for the nightclub scene tonight. Sarcasm was my natural defense in stressful situations, but this time I wasn't joking. *Honestly Aphrodite, I'm exhausted, so I think I'll pass on that suggestion if you don't mind.*

You can sleep later. Listen carefully, Adonis, because this is important. Drive back to Paphos, and park at your hotel. Walk three blocks after turning right out of the lobby, and then take a small street that looks like an alley on the left. It's called Artemis Lane. Caduceus will be on your right, two blocks in. You can't miss it. Ask for the owner. He's expecting you.

He's expecting me?

Yes. He knows all about you and that if you turned out to be who I hoped you'd be that we would need his professional help. You have an appointment.

What kind of nightclub owner took appointments in the middle of the night? I answered my own question with half-serious paranoia, imagining some scar-faced gangster who would appreciate having my feet already fixed in quick-dry cement for my imminent swim with the fishes. *Who in the world are you sending me to? This whole thing just seems a little bit out of the ordinary.*

He's a good friend of mine, who wears many hats. Your appointment is at 2:45, and it's almost 1:30. You'd better get going. I opened my figurative mouth to speak, but she cut me off. *No arguments. And there's something else.*

What now.

44

Caduceus is a private club that allows entry by invitation only. You'll need a password.

Lay it on me. Irreverent nonchalance was yet *another* one of my coping mechanisms. This was becoming very 'cloak and dagger' very quickly, and quite frankly, I was feeling more than a little bit nervous.

It's Elysium.

Won't 'Heaven' do?

No, Adonis. Why would it?

Because the two words are interchangeable.

She sighed. *The password is Elysium-not Heaven, Nirvana, Eden, or Cloud Nine. See you in Polis, love. Dream about me!* And instantly, she was gone, just like that, vanishing into thin air without even the faintest hint of stage-drama. Where was the smoke, the lightning flashes, the thunderclaps, or the explosions? There had been no warning whatsoever; and here I was, still trapped in this damnable stone column...

Or was I? Just as abruptly as she had disappeared, I realized that I had somehow been released. I stretched my arms, confirming that I was no longer encased in stone. "Feels good," I murmured, as I found my way back to the rope ladder and started climbing down. Had this really happened, or was it only a dream? I pinched myself when I reached the bottom but since I didn't wake up, I decided that I would have to accept the situation and simply run with it.

I retraced my steps from earlier that night until I finally made it back to the main road, which would eventually lead me to Caduceus, where I hoped to finally get some answers! But who was I kidding, really? I had no bargaining chip, no cards to play, and no trick up my sleeve-which meant, I realized apprehensively as I climbed into my car, that I was (in every sense of the phrase) 'at her mercy'.

Chapter 5
Hypnotic Suggestion

My watch read *2:30 am*, and the streets were deserted. Her directions were accurate; and a few minutes later, I found myself standing in front of a tastefully adorned and sophisticated looking jazz club, which seemed strikingly out of place on the quiet backstreet. The poster tacked on the door advertised the night's entertainment: *Eros and Eos*, featuring a partially-clad and very attractive blonde (presumably Eos) lying on top of a piano, microphone in hand; and a handsome piano player (Eros) sporting a stylishly unkempt hairstyle. Not surprisingly, the musician seemed to have one eye on his sheet music and the other on his partner's cleavage.

What strange stage names for a musical duet, I thought; but it was certainly imaginative, and indisputably suitable for a city where mythological references seemed to pop up at every turn. Eros, of course, was the Greek deity also known as Cupid; and Eos was the Titan goddess of the dawn, cursed with eternal sexual promiscuity by an ever-jealous Aphrodite because of an affair she had had with Aphrodite's love-interest at the time, Ares.

I stepped up to the door, taking in all of the references to Hermes, another one of the major Greek deities, at once. First, located just above the doorframe, I noticed a gold sculpted rendering of the Messenger god, caught as if frozen in mid-flight-his winged heels somehow providing magical

47

propulsion, his athlete's body sleek and muscular, and his symbolic wand (the caduceus staff, of course) gripped in his left hand. An inscription, engraved in small cursive lettering beneath the metal miniature, piqued my curiosity. Backing up half a step, I peered upward, squinting in the dim lamplight so that I could read the tiny words inscribed in a sweeping arc below the hovering crafted sculpture.

Muse-sing of Hermes, the luck-bringing messenger of the Gods. You are a bringer of dreams, a watcher by night, and a consort to all mortals and immortals. Hail, Mercury: guide and giver of grace and good things; turn ye now to another song!

It was 'The Homeric Hymn to Hermes'. How appropriate that I would be directed to seek guidance at a nightclub that referenced the patron god of wanderers, travelers, vagabonds, and thieves. I definitely felt like I was on the run, so perhaps the owner of this nightclub would be just the right person to give me sanctuary.

Next, the doorknob was actually fashioned in the form of Hermes' staff: the caduceus, which he was often pictured holding in representations of him in art and sculpture. A plaque, centered below a brass peephole, announced that patrons were allowed entry by invitation only, and that all potential customers should ring first, which I started to do until I noticed another discretely placed, smaller plaque that was located just above the doorbell. I leaned forward in order to get close enough to read what it said. *Mercutio Hermes,*

Attorney at Law, the tiny print stated. *Legal clients please use the back entrance.*

So, Aphrodite's 'friend' was an attorney, who just happened to be named Hermes, and who undoubtedly owned the Caduceus Club as well. Why should that surprise me? She had said, after all, that he 'wore many hats.' One coincidence after the other after the other didn't seem to bother me even a tiny bit at this point; so if I had been steered by the goddess of love to the office of a public defender who also shared the name of one of the original twelve Greek deities, then so be it. With a shrug, I rang the bell.

My call was answered quickly from inside, but only after I had been thoroughly inspected, I felt sure, from the other side of the viewing hole. I heard the mechanical sound of iron on steel that indicated that the locking mechanism was being disarmed, and then the door opened slightly.

"Can I help you?" I could only see one squinting eye and half of a nose through the crack in the partially opened doorway.

"I hope so," I replied. "The password is *Elysium.*"

It worked because the door opened fully in response, revealing a slim man in his early sixties, dressed in a tuxedo. "We've been expecting you."

"You have?"

"Of course we have. Right this way, sir." I was immediately ushered through the doorway and directly into a dimly-lit room that looked strangely familiar. Just like my favorite club in New Haven, it was just large enough to seat an intimate crowd of thirty or so at a selection of small tables scattered restaurant-style across the floor-all of them occupied, except for one in the back corner. Stool-seating at a small bar across the room was also full, I noticed. It could have been an exact replica of my hang-out just off Yale's campus, which just goes to show that some things, regardless of the country or culture, are strangely universal. All eyes were glued on the brightly illuminated stage in front and the 'live-and-in-person' versions of the poster advertisement out front.

"It's late," the woman lying on the grand piano was saying, her voice low and sultry, "but we have time for one more number." Her head was propped on a bent elbow, causing her bleached-blonde hair to cascade over her shoulders with a kiss of contrast onto the shiny black mahogany. She held a microphone up to her glossy lips, which were painted the same shade of crimson red as her glittery sequined dress-cut so high that her smooth, bare legs reached all the way to her upper thigh, deliciously pushing the boundaries of discretion. "Thank you so very much for coming out tonight. I'm Eros and he's Eos, ladies and gentlemen. We'll be here again tomorrow, for all of you who seek and crave love."

Eros started playing, the notes of generic introduction eventually transitioning with lazy expertise into the first few bars of Sinatra's *My Funny Valentine*, Cupid's crystal blue eyes lingering every so often (or more) on his partner's décolletage-a fixation that had also been captured in the billboard photo outside. Then she started singing, and it was nothing less than hypnotic. I listened, enthralled, as she sang the first verse and then the chorus, her smoky demeanor more than subtly suggestive, leading my thoughts into places that moaned with private ecstasy and screamed with hidden desires; and by the time she got to the line that referenced Greek 'figures', I had totally lost myself in the vocal, and visual, seduction-so much so that the sudden tap on my shoulder caused me startle like a sleepwalker jolted out of a walking fantasy.

Looking around, I noticed with embarrassment that I had unknowingly wandered into the middle of the seating area. "I'm so sorry," I apologized to the hostess, who seemed to have materialized right next to me, although she had probably been standing there all along. "Her voice is captivating."

She laughed softly. "Eos has that effect on people; she kind of gets into your head, if you know what I mean. You're not the only one, just look around!"

Sure enough, Eos had managed to mentally 'capture' every single person in the room. In fact, the young couple seated immediately behind me didn't even seem to realize that I was standing right in front of them, completely obscuring their view.

"Would you like to be seated?" Her tone was familiar, not formal, as if she were addressing a friend rather than a customer.

I cleared my throat. "I'm actually looking for someone. Is the owner around? My friend told me to ask for him."

She smiled knowingly. "My brother has been expecting you." I must have looked baffled, so she hurried to explain. "Well, half-brother. We have different mothers, but were both fathered by Zeus."

My jaw literally dropped. I was quite familiar with the mythological family tree. Apollo and Artemis were twins born from the same mother: the Titan goddess Leto; and they had two half-brothers: Dionysus... and Hermes. "If Hermes is your brother," I stuttered, quickly making the obvious connection, "then you must be Artemis?"

"Of course I am, silly. Follow me; you can wait back here, at your reserved table."

"So you *know* me, then?" I asked as she led me to the empty table that I had noticed a few moments before.

"Of course I do. *Everyone* does. When Aphrodite called to arrange your appointment, we could hardly believe it was true. But here you are, and there's no mistaking you. We're all so happy you're back, Adonis!" She touched my arm, helping me gently to sit, and then bent down, her face close to mine looking concerned and serious. "About the boar-you know I didn't send him." It took a moment to register, but when it did I nodded, and she responded with a deep sigh of relief. "Rumors in this community are so difficult to dispel. I *never* felt threatened by your hunting skills, Adonis. It was Ares who killed you, in a jealous rage, because of his feelings for Aphrodite."

"I know" was all I could manage to say, but it was apparently enough because her face brightened. "I'm so relieved. None of us knew what was going through your mind at that terrible moment, and I've worried for centuries that maybe you blamed me."

"No, never," I responded, because let's face it-how could I have blamed *anyone* for something that I was pretty sure had never really happened? I felt very much like Scrooge in *The Christmas Carol*, who attributed his encounter with Jacob Marley, at first, to 'an undigested bit of meat' causing a fitful sleep and an exceptionally realistic nightmare.

"Good. Now let me get Hermes." She turned on a high-heel and walked purposefully across the floor, passing the stage to her right and disappearing behind a curtained-door.

A waitress brought me a drink, even though I hadn't ordered one. "Single-malt Islay Scotch, aged 18 years-your favorite. It's on the house," she said, placing the glass in front of me with a wink. I guess she knew me too, but at this point I decided it was probably in my best interest to stop asking. It had been a long, long night, and something told me it wasn't even *close* to being over.

I gratefully took a sip of the whisky, and then another, and then another; and then decided 'what the hell', draining the entire contents of the glass in one gulp. It seemed like the best remedy for all the craziness I had witnessed so far (and everything yet to come), so I nonchalantly signaled the waitress for another one, my eyes watering and my throat still burning from glass number one. Almost instantly, she returned with round two; and at that same moment, a man emerged from the back room, coming out the same way Artemis had gone in.

Even though I saw him with eyes that were starting to swim from the effects of the hastily consumed alcohol, I recognized him immediately-or at least I thought I did. Wasn't he my friend and colleague from Yale, Reginald Winks?

"Reggie!" I called out loudly, getting more than a few puzzled looks from the audience in my immediate vicinity. Wasn't he Reggie? While this unresolved question lingered in the air, he seemed to be doing *exactly* the same thing: hovering, to be exact, with his feet floating an inch or two off the floor, propelled by some invisible force that caused him to close the gap between us much more quickly than was humanly possible. Were those tiny wings protruding from his heels? I could *swear* they were; and he was wearing shoes with no socks, specifically to accommodate them.

"Reggie?" I repeated when he had finally arrived.

"No, old chap; I'm Mercutio Hermes. Welcome to *Caduceus,* old boy."

"I'm sorry, but you look exactly like a close friend of mine."

He took the empty seat across from me at the table-the same one, I suddenly realized, that I had just shared with Reggie a day or so ago at the duplicate club in Connecticut. "I just have one of those faces," he explained, offering me his hand, which I took and shook a little bit suspiciously-because he *did* look just like Reggie. Tall and lean, he had my friend's jet-black hair cropped short on the sides, the same coal grey eyes, and a similar demeanor: outwardly aloof; but once 'inside', the select few would find a friend for life. He and Reggie also seemed to share the same taste in clothes, from his tailored silk shirt right down to his Gucci shoes, the avant-garde black and grey reflecting a style that some might consider pretentious.

"I must say, you haven't changed a bit," he commented in the same slightly muted British accent that Reggie always used. "Two and a half millennia have treated you kindly," he commented, looking me up and down. "Granted, you have been cycled and re-cycled through endless births, deaths and re-births, but you have certainly weathered the process well."

I must have looked bewildered. He patted my arm to reassure me as he sipped from a drink that had miraculously appeared on the table in front of him. "Aphrodite said you wouldn't remember," he said nonchalantly, as he sipped what looked like a vodka martini. "Don't worry, old friend; I'll explain it all momentarily."

Eos had finished the Sinatra number. She blew a kiss into the audience, slid seductively off the piano, adjusted the front of her dress suggestively, and stood with Eros to take a bow. They were rewarded with an enthusiastic round of applause, which tapered and ended when the stage lights dimmed; and before I knew it, they were both seated at the table with us. They suddenly had drinks, too, compliments of the same invisible waitress that had just served Hermes.

"It's *so* exciting to see you again, Adonis," Eos purred. "We've been expecting you for centuries, and now here you are!"

"I'm glad Aphrodite finally found you," Eros (aka Cupid) added. His slight build, soft features, perfectly styled hair, and manicured nails gave him an appearance that definitely favored the feminine side of masculine. "She knew it was you, from the very start."

"Okay, I understand that I'm Adonis, somehow-as unbelievable as that sounds."

"You *are* Adonis," all three of them, in unison, responded.

"If you say so; but explain it to me then, because from where I'm sitting, it doesn't quite add up." Hermes raised an eyebrow but didn't say a word, urging me on with unspoken amusement. "You see," I continued as calmly as I could under the circumstances, "my given name *is* Adonis, I'll give you that; but I *couldn't* be the real one. I'm Adonis James Broussard, known to my friends as 'Jamie'-born in 1975 in New Orleans with a birth certificate to prove it. I'm a tenured professor at Yale University with a PhD in Anthropology, *not* an annually-renewing, every youthful vegetation god fabricated by an ancient myth-driven culture as a symbol of life, death and rebirth."

Hermes put down his glass, motioning for the waitress with a subtle gesture. She seemed to understand the command; and a moment later, the last nightclub patron had been escorted out the door. Hermes stretched his legs, obviously in no rush to fill me in, kicking off his five-hundred dollar shoes, one at a time, to expose his two bare feet. As he wiggled his toes, two feathery ankle wings fanned themselves back and forth at the same time, grateful to be liberated. "They love their freedom, you know," he remarked in a conspiratorial whisper. "Well now-where were we?"

"I'm Adonis, remember?" I decided to use a legal metaphor, which seemed apt given my host's profession. "If the 'accused' is guilty, all he is asking is for his counsel to detail the charges."

My comment had been intended tongue-in-cheek, but little did I know that unintentionally, I had actually stumbled on the truth. Hermes winked. "Since I actually *have* been retained in that capacity, I agree that my client deserves full disclosure."

"You *are* my attorney?" Don't ask me why I was surprised, because by now, everything I had seen and done on this crazy island should have totally eliminated any potential for that kind of reaction.

"Aphrodite arranged it."

"I figured." My motto from here on out, I decided, would be 'expect the unexpected'.

"Now listen carefully, Adonis-here's the scoop. After Aphrodite left you alone in the forest that day, she learned that Ares was planning on ambushing you disguised as a boar." He brushed off his lapel with his fingernails in the universal gesture of self-congratulation. "*I* actually informed her."

"Thanks."

"Don't even mention it. You see, I overhead Ares and Dionysus conspiring together. The pair of them were drunk as skunks, and neither of them had a clue that I was nearby. Equally jealous of you, they pledged that they would see you dead. If Ares didn't succeed as a boar, Dionysus would attack you later after morphing himself into a goat."

"But weren't you in love with her, too?" I knew mythology like the back of my hand. Hermes (and every other god with a Y chromosome) had been enamored with the stunning goddess of love; but Aphrodite and Hermes' 'fling' couldn't have been just a flash in the pan, because their relationship had produced a child with the blended name 'Hermaphrodite'. On the other hand, fathering a baby in the mythological world simply didn't hold the same significance of commitment as it did in *real* society. The Greek gods lived and breathed a magnified soap-opera existence where everyone slept with anyone, and bastard children outnumbered the legitimate by fifty-to-one. Still, love was love. "Eliminating me would work for *all* of Aphrodite's scorned lovers," I commented soberly, "including you."

He shook his head. "I was over her. When I saw how deeply she loved you, I gave her my heartfelt blessing. I wanted things to work out for the two of you."

"My mother had finally found happiness with you, Adonis." Eros, of course, was Aphrodite's son by an unknown father-although some said Hermes planted *that* seed in Aphrodite as well. I looked from Hermes to Cupid and back again, seeing no family resemblance at all, and noticing no 'father and son' connection whatsoever in the way they interacted, so far. Mythological lineage was so complex and convoluted that 'who', exactly, was related to 'whom' often took the form of a puzzle, with pieces that never quite fit together.

Eros sighed. "Everyone deserves to be with their one true love. Touring as a part of this musical duo has really taken its toll on me, from a domestic standpoint. I miss my sweet Psyche. If I didn't need the money, I'd be home with her right now in our cozy little bungalow on the edge of the woods, holding her tight in my arms in our own comfortable featherbed."

I recalled the myth of Eros and Psyche, originally told by Platonicus in *Metamorphoses*, but eventually making its way into more modern fables like *Beauty and the Beast*. According to the legend, Aphrodite, jealous of Psyche's beauty, commands her son Eros to use his godly powers of romantic suggestion to cause her 'competitor' to become enamored with someone ugly. When Eros sees Psyche, he falls instantly in love with her and cannot follow through with his assignment. Instead, he lures Psyche to a lonely cottage in the countryside where he defies his mother and takes Psyche for his wife in secret, making love to her every night in the darkness, but demanding that she never try to see his face. After becoming pregnant, Psyche begins to worry that the man she had married is actually a monster, and that her unborn baby will be hideous, too; so in the middle of the night she lights a lamp while Eros is sleeping, expecting to see something repulsive but discovering the gorgeous Cupid lying there asleep instead. Eros, startled and angry, flees, prompting Psyche to petition for her mother-in-law's help in finding him. To make a long story short, the tale ends happily after Psyche successfully completes a variety of tasks designed to test her worthiness, and is eventually allowed to become reunited eternally with her long lost love.

Eos squirmed slightly in her chair. "I wish I could find someone too. I've been hexed with this eternal curse of sexual promiscuity, and that means I can't settle down with *anyone*, as long as I'm being controlled by this unrestrained urge to bed-hop."

"Patience, Eos," Hermes assured her. "Aphrodite placed that curse on you, and she promised to remove it when she sees you next. If all goes well, you'll not only have the man of your dreams by the end of the week, but for the first time in a millennia you'll have the capacity to remain faithful to him as well!"

"That Ares is the ultimate hunk," Eos cooed. "Do you think he'll really be mine?"

"Relax," Eros reassured her. "We have this completely under control."

It seemed they had wandered off onto some digressing pathway, so I tried to get them back on track. "So Hermes: you were saying that you told Aphrodite about Ares' plan to murder me?"

"Yes, I did; but unfortunately it was too late to stop him, so Aphrodite went straight to Zeus instead, and pleaded with him to intervene somehow."

"I guess he refused, since I'm assuming I died." Suddenly, I realized that I was no longer questioning my identity. However implausible, I was now completely convinced that this fantasy was actually reality.

"Yes and no," Hermes said. "Zeus frowned on Aphrodite's own hyper-sexuality. After all, she was married to one of Zeus' sons, Hephaestus, but was openly unfaithful to him with his *other* son with Hera: Ares. It's not like she was the *only* deity to ignore her wedding vows; but regardless, the countless number of affairs, trysts, and flings notched on Aphrodite's ever-open chastity belt irked 'the all-mighty' to no end."

"Not to mention that all of her children were born out of wedlock-like me," Cupid inserted. "There must be *hundreds* of us out there."

"Honestly, though," Eos contributed, "she *is* the goddess of love, so what do you expect?"

"I couldn't agree more. Anyway, she begged on her knees for Zeus to have mercy on *you*: her true love, swearing that she would retire from the dating scene once and for all if he would only spare you; and her promise to settle down with you and swear off all the meaningless one-night stands worked-sort of."

"Sort of ?" Needless to say, I was bewildered by the qualifier.

"Well, Zeus made a decision to test her sincerity. He decreed that *yes*, you would die at that moment, at Ares' hand, but that your death would not be permanent. It was an ingenious ruling, really. Tell me again, Adonis, what you said a minute ago, about being a tenured professor at Yale, and *not*... "

He paused, apparently waiting for me to fill in the blank, so I did. "... an annually-renewing, every youthful vegetation god."

"Exactly; so in direct accordance with your mythological persona, Zeus declared that you would be re-born over and over again in a continuous string of mortal lives. Your appearance would remain constant and your soul intact, but you would have no memory of your true identity as you lived through countless and varied human lives. It was Aphrodite's task to find you, and as long as she remained faithful to her love for you, your soul would continue to be re-born through the years and centuries of her searching."

I contemplated this strange arrangement with quiet resignation. The explanation made sense; and more importantly, it felt right. Deep inside, I knew that I was indeed Adonis.

"So, I guess she's been faithful to me for all these years," I murmured. "That certainly explains the conversation she had with Ares tonight. She turned me into a stone column to hide me, referencing her celibacy as she tried to get rid of him."

"Yes, Adonis, she's been ever-faithful to you. She's a changed woman; and now, we just have to get Ares off your back, so that you and Aphrodite can get hitched... but only after all of the contracts have been declared null and void."

"Contracts? What contracts?"

"Heavens, there must be half a dozen of them associated with this ancient affair. Without detailing all of them right now, let's just say that Ares has his *own* arrangement with the old man."

"And that would be?" I prompted, cringing as I prepared myself for the bad news.

"Zeus took away the permanence of your death, which of course enraged the temperamental hot-head. To appease his son, Zeus decreed that if he searched for you, found you, and killed you, your second death at his hands would be final and irreversible."

I gulped. No wonder Aphrodite had panicked when she knew Ares was coming. Jealous and vengeful, Ares would have relished the opportunity to finish what he started twenty-five centuries earlier. Thank the gods that he was so easily distracted by his hormone-infatuated obsession with Aphrodite.

"Do you think he'd really kill me if he found me?" I asked, my voice cracking slightly.

"Of course he would," Hermes said quietly. "I hate to say this about my very own half-brother, but this is just fun and games for the muscle-bound idiot. If he finds you first, he'll kill you-because, of course, you're the one and only obstacle to his own deranged romantic goal. If Aphrodite finds you first, he'll seek out the both of you and finish you off, while Aphrodite looks on helplessly in horror. And finally, if Aphrodite gets in the sack with anyone other than you, *including* her ex-lover Ares himself, your body and spirit will disintegrate back into nothingness. In Ares' twisted mind, this is a win-win situation, no matter how you slice it."

"So, I'm doomed no matter how you look at things." I gazed with depressed resignation into my empty whiskey snifter. "Could I have another drink, please? On second thought, make that two!"

Hermes waived away my concern. "We're all *over* this, Adonis, from every conceivable practical as well as legal angle." He slid a piece of paper across the table, while Eros handed me a pen. "Sign here." Hermes pointed decisively to a black 'X' marking a blank line.

"What, exactly, am I signing?"

"It's a contract, officially engaging me as your attorney. My fees have already been paid, so all I need is your 'John Hancock' to make what needs to be done happen."

Why not? He seemed competent enough; so I downed another dram of whiskey and scribbled my name right next to his finger. It seemed that now my life was literally in Hermes hands.

Chapter 6
A Subliminal Stream Of Consciousness

I slept until 2:30 in the afternoon since I hadn't found the comfort of my hotel bed until 5 AM ; and although Hermes had assured me that I could safely wander about without being discovered by Ares, my harrowing experience at Aphrodite's Temple trumped my newfound friend's well-meaning guarantees. I stayed indoors until cocktail hour, meeting Hermes in the hotel bar at 6:30 PM, just as we had agreed.

"No worries, Adonis," he calmly reassured me over a drink. "She threw Ares off your trail with her unexpected romantic advances. He's been trying unsuccessfully to get her back since she cut him off way back when; and now, he won't be able to think about anything else."

"Do you think he'll try to force himself on her before we can implement your plan?" I asked, as visions of a cornered Aphrodite being overpowered into intimacy by the physical strength of her one-time lover flashed in front of my paranoid eyes.

"Never in a million years. Granted he might try, given the right opportunity, but Aphrodite's not so easy. Case in point: she's very quiet right now, subliminally speaking."

"What do you mean?"

"Simply that she's being extra cautious, making sure that even her deepest thought-waves are

thoroughly suppressed. She *adores* you, Adonis."
He gave me a look that said, 'what a cute couple
you make'. "She's jumping through hoops to make
sure you're not discovered by that thick-necked
brute."

I looked thoughtfully into my cocktail, finding
very little reassurance there. "Ares could crush me
like an insect, with one hand tied behind his back
and both eyes closed," I muttered.

"That won't happen."

"You say that because... ?"

"... of *me*. Need I remind you that I'm an
invaluable ally? With the great and powerful 'Oz'
on your side, you're virtually untouchable!"

We would soon see about that; because even
though I was an exceptionally trusting sort, I still
had some lingering doubts about Hermes' true
intentions. "For the life of me, I can't fathom why
you've decided to help me." I was curious to hear
what he would say.

"Well, there's the money, to start." It was hard
to tell whether or not he was joking; but if he
wasn't, I felt oddly reassured. Why? Because cool
hard cash was the most objective motivator I could
imagine. If Aphrodite had bought his loyalty, so be
it, as long as the payment she provided was large
enough to guarantee his loyalty.

"I can live with that. Is that all?"

"Well, the entertainment value is most
definitely an added bonus."

I blinked, staring back at him in disbelief. "Let
me get this straight," I said evenly, leaning forward
for much-needed dramatic emphasis. "So I'm kind
of like the poor slave in one of those public Roman

circuses, amusing the howling audience while the lion chews on one of my limbs and then the other."

He waved away my sarcasm. "Lighten up, old chap-you'll be fine; and when this is all over you'll be reunited with the woman of your dreams in the most happily-ever-after ending imaginable."

"Now that you mention it, this *does* seem like some sort of bizarre fairy-tale."

He ignored my comment, draining his apple martini and glaring at me over the rim of his glass in mock anger. "I must say, you hit way below the belt with that Roman comparison. Those horrid ancient Italians didn't have one single original thought or concept before, during or after their centuries of world domination. They borrowed everything from us, including their roster of deities. If they tried to pull that kind of stunt today, we'd sue them for plagiarism!" He cleared his throat. "What I *meant* to say is that it will be deliciously amusing to see Ares defeated by his own testosterone-inflated sexuality."

"I could be mistaken, but was that some sort of back-handed apology?"

He shrugged noncommittally. "Call it what you like." He looked thoughtfully at me from across the table for a moment, and then leaned forward as if he was preparing to share a safely guarded secret. "He's not all bad, really. Take my word for it-I grew up with the guy. He's extremely obstinate, and not very insightful. Combine those two attributes with an irrational focus on the past, and you get a freight train that'll stop at nothing to regain what he had with Aphrodite before you stepped into the picture and stole his girl."

"I sense just a touch, or more, of brotherly sympathy."

He ignored me, speaking under his breath as if he were having a private conversation with himself. "We were never close as kids, or as adults for that matter; but you can't help feeling sad for the guy, whether you're related to him or not. Anyone with even a minute crumb of common sense would see that Aphrodite's love for him died eons ago. To put it bluntly, she doesn't want him anymore, and you can't force someone to love you."

"So true," I contributed soberly.

"Of course it doesn't help that he hangs out with the old-timers on Mount Olympus."

"In Greece?"

"It's not in Greece, my boy; it's right here, in Cyprus."

"You can't be serious!"

"Why wouldn't I be? Mount Olympus is the highest point on this island, soaring to 1,952 meters. It's located in the center of the Troodos mountain range. Google it."

"Hmm. I never knew there was a Mount Olympus in Cyprus, or that the council of twelve lived here, rather than in Greece."

"Well believe it. Most of the old-timers like Zeus, Poseidon, Hades, and Hera are still up there, stuck in some kind of a time warp, twiddling their thumbs and roughing it on that cold and dreary mountaintop."

"Are they exposed to the elements?" I had always assumed that they had a palace, or something equivalent, to use for accommodations, but what did I know?

"Oh, they're comfortable enough. You see, the facility was recently renovated. To each his or her own, I guess, but if you ask me, it's much more fun to blend and integrate into modern society, as you and I have done-wouldn't you say?"

"I hadn't really thought of myself like that, until now." I was a god who had lived as a mortal for what seemed like forever, and I couldn't really say that I had even a single complaint-that I could recall, at least. "I wish I could remember more than fleeting snatches from my past, though."

He glanced at me knowingly. "That's all part of Zeus' ruling. Your memories will rush back, I assure you, when you're officially instated by 'Pop', at the hearing."

"What do you mean a hearing?"

"I'm going to represent you, remember? We have to make *all* of the contracts involving you, Aphrodite and Ares null and void."

"And how, exactly, are we going to do that?"

"It's complicated." He stirred the remnants of his second drink with a swizzle stick. "Aphrodite will explain when you see her at the Baths in Polis tomorrow."

"Why don't *you* explain it to me *now*?"

"I'm not being intentionally evasive. It's just that I promised Aphrodite that she'd be the one to fill you in on some of the most crucial fine points. Anyway, hearing things from her perspective will be very useful."

"But... "

"A promise is a promise." He stood, yawning. "You've got a two or three hour drive ahead of you tomorrow, and you should get an early start." I stood too, and he gave me his hand. "Good night, friend. If you're as tired as I am, you'll be in dreamland as soon as your head hits the pillow."

"You've got that right." I gripped his palm, but the briefest of handshakes was cut even shorter by his sudden disappearance; so there I was, shaking thin air like some kind of an idiot, while I told myself that it was high time I get used to these magical comings and goings. Sure, it was bad enough that I was taken unawares yet again, and that I had to finish my drink alone; but to make matters worse, his departure via an invisible backdoor meant that I was stuck with the entire bar tab.

Chapter 7
A Mental Trip

I left the next morning for Polis and arrived there exactly three hours later, just as Hermes had predicted, and now I stood now at the registration desk of the hotel near the monastery that Aphrodite had recommended. Before I could say a word, the attractive reception clerk standing across from me on the other side of the counter greeted me with a comfortable familiarity.

"Ah, here you are, finally! We've been expecting you. Welcome to *Hotel Anchises*." I smiled at yet another irony, wondering whether it was simple coincidence that I would be staying at a hotel named after Aphrodite's only mortal lover. "I won't say your real name out loud," she whispered, "since 'you-know-who' may be listening." She smiled and brushed some fragrant wisps of strawberry-blonde hair from her delicate forehead, in a way that said, 'you and I were previously intimate.' Okay, so she was obviously one of 'them'; and judging from her batting eyelashes, she was probably one of my 'ex's', as well-but which one, exactly? Since I seemed to still have amnesia to most everything from the past, I had no choice but to ask.

"Do I know you?"

She bit her lower lip in a most inviting way. "I know you don't remember, but you and I had a fling together in a *very* hot place, a long, long time ago!"

"Persephone!" How could I forget the wild secrecy every winter, sneaking around right under her husband's nose until springtime came and I'd emerge from the Underworld, privately satiated by Hades' consort, to spend the rest of the year in Aphrodite's loving and never-jealous embrace.

"The one and only!" she replied, reaching across the counter to touch my hand. When she didn't withdraw it I felt kind of awkward, because naturally, things had changed. I was pledged to Aphrodite now, and this was a modern promise that I had no intention of breaking.

"You guys are everywhere!" Maybe I would be able to derail an impending advance with some generic banter. "Who will I run into next?" Perhaps the porter and the concierge were also deities in disguise?

She giggled. "You'd be surprised how many of us have seamlessly blended into modern-day society. Major and minor Greek, Egyptian, Norse, and Celtic gods; legendary heroes from all four continents; half-breed immortals and reformed monsters-you name it, they're all out there, quietly living side by side in peaceful harmony with their mortal companions, friends and co-workers. We recently eliminated all of the ancient geographical borders, too." She smiled. "Personally, I've thought about moving to Cincinnati, but it's tough breaking the ties that bind me to Cyprus and Greece."

I raised my eyebrows, uncertain whether to believe her or not. "Cincinnati?"

She removed her hair-clip, which released her waist-length hair in a smooth cascade, tumbling softly onto her darkly-tanned shoulders. "I hear their chili will knock your socks off. In fact, if one can believe the rumors, it's endorsed by Hades himself."

"Speaking of your husband, I always felt a little bit guilty about the way we used to marginalize him. Is he still angry?"

"Not at all. It was Zeus' decree that you spend the cold months frolicking underground and under the bedsheets with me, so Hades had no choice but to eventually come to terms with it. He had his *own* fun on the side, anyway, so it's all just water under the bridge over the river Styx, as they say."

"Well give him my best, won't you? Did you hear," I offered, wondering how she would take the news if she still had feelings for me, "that I've settled down with Aphrodite? Or at least that's our plan."

She put me at ease with her smile. "Of course, and you have my blessing. I conceded to Aphrodite long ago, well in advance of your untimely death. Although we had a blast every time you visited, I could see that you were secretly itching to get back to her. You were so obviously in love with her, and her with you, that I petitioned Zeus to end our arrangement. That was, let's see, three-thousand or so years ago?"

"I didn't realize. Thank you."

"Don't even mention it. You two were so adorable together, and you definitely brought out the best in her-because no one else, before you, had been able to even come *close* to reigning in her wildness. I felt her pain like my own, really, when you were murdered by that brute."

72

"I'm remembering tidbits here and there, but nothing complete. It's frustrating. I feel like an absolute idiot, you know."

As she gazed with brilliant aquamarine eyes directly into mine, I could understand how a guy could easily fall for her, like I apparently did, if only half-heartedly. "You'll remember it all, after the hearing," she said, reaching under the counter for something as she spoke. "Here." She handed me not only a card-key, but a folded piece of paper as well. "It's a note from Aphrodite."

"Thanks Persephone. See you soon?"

"Sure. We can double-date, the four of us, once you and your goddess are hitched."

"That would be wonderful."

"Good luck, Romeo. We're all rooting for you!"

I turned away, picked up my luggage, and walked towards the elevator, opening the note on the way. The words were written in the same flowery cursive as the previous message that I had received while waiting for Aphrodite at *Taverna Hephaestus*.

Adonis,

These two days have seemed like an eternity to me. I've missed you so-you have no idea how much.

I can't wait to see you tonight, but we're still in danger. Our contact will have to be very brief, I'm afraid. Ares has been incredibly persistent, but I've been able to elude him so far. I think our plan will work, but until Ares is safely out of the way, we have to be very careful.

Meet me at the Baths, at midnight sharp. Until then, keep a very low profile.

I'm yours forever, darling.
Your one and only,
Aphrodite.

I folded the note, kissed it tenderly, slipped it into my shirt pocket, and stepped into the elevator. Once in my room, I flopped face down on the bed; and as I started to drift off, it occurred to me that all I did with my downtime on this strange vacation was sleep, but I couldn't help it. A moment later, I was out.

Chapter 8
A Lucid Dream

I could see easily since the waning moon was only three nights beyond full, shining brightly at the pinnacle of a clear night sky that was stippled with thousands of glittering stars. I walked alone passed the ruins of the monastery and around the far end of the partially reconstructed tourist attraction. The gate securing Aphrodite's bath was low, hardly representing a barrier at all, so I had no difficulty whatsoever climbing over to the other side, finding myself on a small pathway sheltered by an arbor, which was covered completely with climbing vines and speckled with countless white flowers. The 'Baths', located just ten meters or less from the pathway's origin at the gate, should have been re-named in the singular. I stood looking at a solitary pond that I recalled well, fed primarily by an underground spring with some small amount of supplemental water-volume contributed by a trickling stream that skimmed its way over a bed of down-sloping rocks to end with barely a splash in the far-side of the magical pool.

I sat on a stone bench next to the water, checking my watch to confirm that I had arrived just a few minutes before midnight. When the minute hand told me it was time, I closed my eyes, and a moment later I sensed her gentle materialization right next to me.

"Am I dreaming?"

"Don't you know you *can't* be, precisely because you asked that question?"

I realized that she was probably right, because a dreamer is almost *never* aware that he or she is dreaming. I had heard of exceptions, though. "This could be one of those 'lucid' dreams."

"Nonsense. You're as lucid as I am, my darling." She touched my hand briefly, and then withdrew it. "See? Don't I feel 'real' to you?"

I responded by opening my eyes. "Yes," I managed to say, reaching towards her with the intention of taking her in my arms, but she wouldn't let me. Instead she stood up abruptly and moved a few paces away.

"It's much too dangerous, Adonis. Ares will sense my emotion again if you hold me, or if we kiss. Let's not have a repeat of that temple fiasco-agreed?"

"Agreed. After tomorrow, though?"

"Yes, I hope so. Now close your eyes again while I undress and get in."

I did, but not completely (who could blame me?), which meant that I got an unadulterated view, through an eyelid slit, of her glorious naked backside as she let her toga slide provocatively to the ground. I watched with my heart literally pounding as she tested the water with a delicate toe, waded into the pond passed her thighs, and then turned unawares to face me while she slowly lowered herself into the water, her wet skin glistening in the moonlight, until she was eventually submerged up to her delicate collarbones.

I gulped, more loudly than intended. "Were you peeking?"

"Maybe."

"You're bad; but then again, you always *have* been."

"What can I say, except that people never change, even after a few dozen centuries." I heard the gentle splash of water, still watching through disingenuous eyelids while she used cupped hands to wet her face and soak her rich, walnut hair. "I have two questions."

"Shoot."

"First of all, can I open my eyes now; and second, would it be okay for me to join you in there, just like I did a few millennia ago?"

"'Yes' to number one, and definitely 'no' to number two. If you came in here with me we would have a repeat of our first meeting. I couldn't resist you then, so why do you think I'd be able to now?"

"But I could just wade in there quietly and sit next to you, my intentions as innocent as a child's."

"You are *not* innocent, and never had child-like intentions even when you *were* one! Even if we had the willpower to sit naked next to each other and not take it to the next level, he would sense my hormones surge. We've been there and done that, in Paphos-remember? We don't want to 'summon' Ares, now do we?"

"Of course not; it's just that this is very difficult. I can't wait for this to be over with, tomorrow."

"Except that it *won't* be, entirely, until the hearing on Mount Olympus."

"Don't you think it's high time that someone filled me in, completely? As an FYI, Hermes left most of the 'explaining' to you, for some reason."

77

"I'm fully aware of that; so right now, you'll be getting the complete 'skinny'... "

"... from a very sexy skinny-dipper, no less?"

She smiled "The pun, you should know, was *entirely* intended."

"Very witty. Go on, my bathing beauty."

"Alright; so when Zeus decreed that you wouldn't truly die, he also stipulated that your identity could be 'made-over' from mortal to god, but *only* if five requirements were satisfied."

"Hold on. I thought Adonis *was* a god."

"Well, there's actually considerable confusion about that. Some say he's a fertility god; but remember, your mother was the *mortal* princess, Smyrna, who conceived you by seducing her *mortal* father, Theias, the king of Syria."

"So if my parents were mortal... "

"... then you are too, at least according to most authorities."

"My birth, though, was nothing less than magical. Doesn't that count for *something*?" Instead of the usual labor-room delivery, my nine months of woody gestation ended when I was ejected out of the hollow trunk of the myrrh tree that my mother had been transformed into, as punishment for her incestuous indiscretions.

"I'm afraid that counts for considerably *less* than something! 'Nature' always supersedes 'nurture' in the deity regulations manual."

"But how is it, then, that a mere mortal like me developed the status as a god-like representation of life, death and rebirth?"

"You didn't always have that reputation until you actually *lived* that reality."

"How so?"

"Well, it wasn't until Zeus ruled that you would be constantly 'recycled' through countless mortal lives on that day of your 'death' so long ago, that you basically became the annually-renewing fertility symbol that everyone associates you with."

"Okay, I get it. So I'm human rather than divine; but you said that could change, if five requirements were fulfilled?"

"Yep."

"Care to share?"

She held up her index finger. "First I would have to find you, in defiance of all the complexities of space, time and geography."

"And here I am. The first condition has been satisfied."

"Correct." She raised her thumb on the same hand. "Second, I would have to remain true to you up until the day of our reunion, swearing off all other lovers, suitors, one night stands, and would-be bedtime companions."

"You've done that too, I assume-otherwise I would have disintegrated into thin air at the first moment you were unfaithful. I know that much already, from talking to Hermes."

"Next," (her third finger went up) "you would have to make it to the hearing without being discovered and killed by Ares, because he can make your death final and irrevocable by slaughtering you again, at any given time prior to the legal proceedings."

"I get that. So far you haven't told me anything that I don't already know."

She put up another finger. "Number four, you'll have to plead your case in the courtroom, convincing Zeus not only that you deserve me, but that you deserve the promotion from mortal to god."

"That doesn't sound very difficult," I said hopefully. "Will it be?"

"I'm not sure. It depends a little bit on Zeus' mood at the time. He's very volatile, which means that sometimes his rulings are arbitrary and illogical. Plus, he's gotten more and more feeble these past five or six centuries-a touch of senior dementia setting in, if you ask me."

"That doesn't sound so good."

"Well, remember you'll have Hermes arguing with you. He's an excellent attorney."

"I don't like this uncertainty. Do you mean to tell me that Zeus could very well decide that you and I should be kept apart?"

"Unfortunately, yes. But much worse than that, he could decide that you shouldn't get the promotion; in which case... "

I looked at her expectantly. "In which case *what*, exactly?"

She sighed. "Well, I guess it won't help matters to keep this from you. If he rules that you remain mortal, you will disintegrate, right there on the spot. You see, you've lived so many mortal lives by now that your death would of course be immediate. People don't usually live for three thousand years plus, you know."

"Great," I said. "This hearing sounds more like a trial to me, with my death sentence hanging in the balance, depending on an unpredictable and demented judge's whim."

"It'll be okay, Adonis. I'll be there with you, every step of the way."

"You might as well tell me the fifth requirement," I said. "It couldn't be any worse than the fourth.

She smiled, holding up all five fingers. "The last one is easy. You have to agree to an immediate marriage ceremony, with Zeus presiding as Justice of the Peace, should he rule in our favor rather than with the prosecution."

"You're right-that one's easy. We're both unattached." Then something occurred to me. "We *are* both unattached, aren't we?" I wouldn't put it past these god-types to have more than one 'official' husband or wife. Did they divorce, like humans did; or did their spouses accumulate like a jealous harem instead, with each and every member jockeying, every so often, for premiere status?

She knew immediately what I was thinking. "Do you mean Hephaestus?"

"Well, he *is* your mythological spouse, and there's no mention anywhere in the stories about a formal dissolution of your marriage vows."

She snorted. "That arranged marriage was doomed from day one."

"Obviously; but are you *divorced*, rather than just separated?"

"Of *course* we are! Zeus released me from that contrived and awkward commitment a long time ago, right after Ares and I were caught in that net that Hephaestus dropped on us in my bedroom. I think the old guy felt guilty that he had forced me into a loveless marriage, and to this day I'm convinced that the quick-and-easy annulment he

81

granted me was in actuality a backdoor apology. I'm grateful he didn't put me through the usual rigmarole of official divorce proceedings before the Olympian council."

"So, you're single then?"

"Unhitched, but itching *not* to be." She turned her face up towards the stars. "It's our destiny, Adonis, to be together."

We didn't speak for a moment, but that was fine because there were no words, anyway, to describe the exhilaration I felt. "It's so fantastic to be alive," I finally declared.

"And we need to *keep* you that way. Really, I should probably go now."

"So soon?"

"Unfortunately, yes. If I don't keep moving, Ares will eventually pinpoint my location and find out we're together."

"How is that even *possible*?" I asked.

"It's kind of like tracing a phone call. Although I'm suppressing my thought-waves, some of my emissions persist and he can detect them. With enough time, his internal GPS will find me, but if I move to a different location his radar needs to re-boot and then attempt to re-connect."

"Why can't he tune into *my* frequency?" I asked.

"You and he don't have the emotional connection required for that kind of synchronization; plus, you're on a different wavelength from the rest of us."

"Meaning?"

"You're not a god, so you're transmitting in the equivalent of an AM radio bandwidth, rather than FM."

"Literally?"

"It's an analogy. You need to be on the same *mental* plane to sense someone's telepathic energy, and you're simply not there yet-but you *will* be, if you end up getting that promotion."

"So that explains why it took so long for you to find me."

"Exactly. It was hit or miss for twenty-five centuries, my love."

"That makes perfect sense." And the strange thing is that it *did* make sense, in the exact same way absolute nonsense seems faultlessly logical in some dreams. For the second time that night, I pushed the thought aside, reminding myself that this kind of sleeper's-awareness almost never occurred. "So when will I see you again?"

"At the arranged lunch at *Demeter's*; and then on to Mount Olympus, after Ares has been dealt with. I'll miss you terribly!"

"Me too," I said, to thin air; because instantly, she was gone.

Chapter 9
A Soporific

"I'm having some second thoughts," I admitted, looking at myself in the mirror and adjusting the final knot and loop of my black silk bowtie.

"Relax." Hermes stood with one foot on a stool to provide easier access to an untied shoelace. "Trust me, this is perfectly safe."

"Are you sure he won't recognize me?"

"Never in a million years." He stood, effortlessly inserting one cufflink and then the other into his shirtsleeves without even looking. In contrast, I was having considerable difficulty with my tuxedo coat. "Let me help you with that."

"I feel like a circus contortionist."

He lifted the left shoulder of my jacket and pulled the sleeve smoothly over my arm. "There." He spun me around and straightened my lapel. "Very becoming."

"Even if you change my appearance, won't Ares be able to detect my mental thought waves?"

"Your 'station' is on a completely different bandwidth. Didn't Aphrodite explain?"

"Yes, but simple logic tells me that tuning into a transmission tower far, far away might be more of a challenge than detecting close-by emissions. For God's sake, I'm going to be right *next* to the guy!"

"It doesn't work like that. He doesn't have a pass-code to access your server, as it were; and even if he did, he'll be so distracted by everything that's going on that he wouldn't notice Zeus himself waiting on him, let alone little old you. Plus, I'll be right there beside you."

I crossed my arms thoughtfully, looking past him from the antechamber into the dining room, where the table had been set for three. "Okay, I get that; but won't Ares sense *your* thought waves, since you share an elite camaraderie?"

"Casting a 'barrier' enchantment is child's play for a god like me. My thoughts will be vaulted away, safe and sound. He'll think I'm a waiter, just like you."

"If it's so easy for you guys to camouflage your thoughts, what went wrong the night I met Aphrodite at the Temple?"

"Two things. First of all, I'm a more powerful deity than she is."

"I'll buy that." Why not? It made perfect sense. As a son of Zeus, one could easily imagine that a god like Hermes could outperform Aphrodite, whose parentage was shrouded in mystery. The most accepted story explaining her origin claims that she was created when Cronus cut off Uranus's genitals and threw them into the sea, causing her to rise out of the resulting 'sea foam'. That particular myth, contending that the goddess of love was 'divinely' conceived out of her father's semen, also explained why she was so 'sexual', given the steamy and potent foundation of her physical make-up. "What's the second reason?"

"She couldn't control the emotional surge that occurred when she kissed you-it's as simple as that."

"So she let her guard down?"

85

"Exactly, but who can blame her? After two and half millennia of celibacy, what do you expect?"

He had an explanation for everything, and I finally felt satisfied. "So, do I get to pick my temporary face?" I asked, walking a few paces to glance at my reflection in the mirror, straightening my hair while Hermes sank smugly into a comfortable appearing overstuffed easy chair.

"Sorry to dash your hopes, 'double-o-seven', but you can't be Daniel Craig for *this* mission." He draped one arm nonchalantly over the back of his seat. "Tonight's escapades require each of us to be exact replicas of the two originals. Ares knows all of the servers here by name, since he's a 'regular', so we both have to be recognizable."

I remained silent since his commentary didn't require a reply, walking over to the open window instead and leaning both hands on the sill. As I looked out, I noticed two waiters, dressed in tuxedos identical to ours, negotiating the winding slope that led from the central building to our secluded dining cottage, wheeling a loaded serving cart between them. "They're coming," I announced over my shoulder to the still-seated Hermes. "Which one am I?"

"You'll be the assistant waiter, of course." Hermes rose to his feet and looked passed me out the window with an expression on his face that reminded me of a witness making an easy identification from a police line-up. "Nikkos and Spiro, just as I expected, which is very good indeed. They are both highly suggestible, if I remember correctly."

"How will you get rid of them?" I moved away from the window to shut the door between the sitting room and the dining area. They would arrive in a minute, and I wasn't sure if Hermes needed to keep us concealed while he decided how to pull this off.

"It'll be 'a piece of cake', as they say. Watch this."

I waited, but nothing happened. "Watch what?" I asked, frowning.

"For your information, this is what they call a 'dramatic pause'. It heightens the effect, you know."

And a split second later, he was gone. "Okay, I'm impressed," I admitted, addressing the empty spot where he had been standing a moment before. "I hope you're still here somewhere, Hermes, because it would be a little bit awkward for me to have to hide in this sitting room looking like my true self when Ares eventually arrives." I gazed towards a small closet with a sigh.

Hermes laughed. "I'm standing right in front of you, and you know it. Wait here while I 'glamour' our two unsuspecting attendants."

"Is that really the proper terminology? You make yourself sound like some kind of a vampire."

"'Glamour', 'mesmerize', 'entrance'-call it what you like, my mortal friend. And just for the record, vampires don't really exist."

"They don't? How about witches, werewolves, shape-shifters, and demons?"

"Nope; just us gods, I'm afraid. This is a discussion for another time, Adonis; but I've got news for you. All of those legends and myths; all of those supernatural beings... "

"What about them?"

"They're all gods in disguise."

"What the hell does *that* mean?"

"Exactly what it sounds like. There are thousands and thousands of gods walking the earth with a whole lot of time on their hands. Sometimes, for fun, they re-create themselves."

"So, in a way, vampires *do* exist," I concluded.

"That depends, really, on how you look at it, I guess. Those creatures are just alternate identities for some very bored and twisted deities." His pause had that contemplative feel, like a psychiatrist sizing up his patient in order to prepare a case summary. "Actually, those guys have serious self-esteem issues. For the life of me, I can't understand why they can't accept themselves for who they are. I *love* being Hermes, and can't *imagine* ever being anyone else. But that's just me I guess."

I heard the outside door open, followed by the rattle of the serving cart being maneuvered and jostled over the threshold. I looked expectantly at the space of air that had been producing the voice of reason, waiting for its occupant's next move. "This will only take a few seconds," whispered my invisible but far from imaginary friend. "Stay put while I send them both home, using an instantaneous and most effective mode of transportation!"

"Remember, Hermes, that you're dealing with a novice over here, whose ignorance knows no bounds; so tell me- if you whisk them away with your magic, won't they wonder about being here one minute, and home the next?"

"No, because they'll have no recollection of ever coming to work today; plus, I'll implant a fictitious phone conversation in their impressionable heads."

"A *phone* conversation?"

"Sure-the one they'll think they had first thing this morning with the restaurant manager, informing them that business is slow today and they won't be needed."

That would work. "Go do it, then. Sometimes I think you're all talk and no action."

"May I remind you that the only reason I'm still standing here is you? *You're* the one with all the burning questions."

"You *love* having an apprentice-admit it!"

"If I've learned anything in this job, it's to admit *nothing*. Wait here, I'll be right back."

"I'm not going anywhere."

A split second later I heard a brief gasp of surprise, followed by the sound of a platter crashing to the floor. A voice that I recognized as Hermes' murmured something softly, in a language that could have been Greek (or just as easily, for that matter, Latin, Macedonian, or Olympian, if such a language even existed); and a second later, the door to the sitting room opened to reveal a smug and satisfied Hermes. He bowed dramatically and with an exaggerated self-complimentary flourish, standing on the other side of the threshold. "Voila. Didn't I tell you that it would be the simplest thing in the world to send them on their merry way? But that was child's play. If you think *that* trick was slick, then watch *this* one!"

He bowed again; and instantly, in the time it took for me to blink, he was no longer Hermes, but an aging and corpulent headwaiter instead. The sudden change in his appearance from slim and dashing to short, pudgy, and balding was so preposterously discordant that it made me burst out laughing.

"Do you think *I* look ridiculous? Just wait until you look at *yourself* in the mirror!"

He spoke with Hermes' voice, and I stifled a guffaw. "For future reference," I advised with tongue in cheek, "it's customary for the ventriloquist to *disguise* his voice when he makes his dummy speak."

He sighed petulantly. "Is this better?" he asked in a deep baritone laced with an almost unintelligible Greek (or was it Turkish?) accent.

"Perfect," I confirmed, following him into the dining room. "Am I Nikko, or Spiro?"

"You're Spiro. And remember, if you talk-which I advise strongly against-disguise *your* voice as well. Ares has a memory like an elephant... "

"... and a mammoth's build to match."

"This is no time for witticisms. If Ares addresses you directly (which he probably won't, since you're only the back waiter) I'll tell him you're recovering from a summer cold and a bout of laryngitis."

I strolled over to a mirror and smiled at the reflection that gazed back at me. I had a head of curly dark hair, a thin pointed nose, and no discernible chin. "I may not be much to look at, but at least I'm young."

"Well, at least I'm a god and not a mortal."

"Touche."

"Ah, Aphrodite's just arrived, so now it's down to business. She's the first wave."

The door opened, and there she was. "Hello boys." She winked at me, somehow knowing which costume was mine. "You just tell me when, and I'll call Ares."

"We need Eros and Eos here before you do that. Remember, you agreed to release the curse of promiscuity that you placed on Eos, so she can offer a sincere proposal of fidelity to Ares. If we can get him to at least *consider* her offer, Eros can make the deal final with his famous arrow."

She leaned against the wall with her arms crossed. "I know that, and I'll do what we agreed. Where are they, anyway? They're late."

Hermes looked at his watch. "They should be arriving just about... *now*." As he spoke, Eros and Eos appeared as if on command, seated in front of their empty plates at the table.

"Hello dearie," Aphrodite said from her standing position, addressing an Eos who gazed back at her with a face scrunched up in obvious suspicion. "Relax, honey. I was a very vindictive and jealous woman in those days, but now I've changed. I should have released your curse *years* ago."

Eos' features visibly softened. "Well if we're speaking candidly, I don't *entirely* regret that spell you cast. One thing for sure is that I've had some heart-pounding adventures because of you; but now,

I'm *more* than ready to settle down. Without these uncontrollable urges, do you think I'll be able to live a normal life, with the man I love? My sights are set on Ares-it's him, or no one."

"He'll be yours, all right," Eros declared. "After I shoot him with my arrow, he'll be like putty in your hands."

"I want Ares to want me for *me*, not because of another hex or enchantment."

"My arrow will simply seal the deal, Eos. Ares had the 'hots' for you years ago, don't you remember? Things didn't work out between the two of you because you hopped in the sack with anything that breathed, *not* because the two of you were incompatible. Ares simply got tired of the humiliation-understandably, in my humble opinion."

"You're right. Without the curse, I think I have a good 'shot' at getting him back." She grinned. "No pun intended."

"So *do* it Aphrodite," Hermes said, tapping his foot impatiently. "We don't have all day."

Aphrodite shrugged. "It's already done. The curse has been lifted, Eos. Congratulations."

Eos looked surprised. "I don't *feel* any different. Do I *look* different to any of you?"

"No," we all said at once.

"The curse gave you a wandering eye, Eos; it never changed your appearance," Aphrodite explained. "You're just as beautiful and irresistible now, even *without* the liberated attitude."

"Ares will adore you," Hermes said dismissively. "Now it's time for step two. Call Ares now, Aphrodite, but be sure you get out of here before he actually arrives."

"Gotcha." Aphrodite closed her eyes, whispering something silently with barely parted lips; and then she disappeared. I blinked twice, because her spot holding up the wall was now occupied by none other than Ares.

"Where is she?" he growled, looking around. "She called me here. Where in Hades name *is* she? I swear I'm gonna *kill* somebody if this is some kind of a trick!"

"Calm down, Ares, and take a seat." Eros motioned with his hand towards the empty place setting. "Aren't you hungry? We've already ordered your lunch."

"I *demand* to see Aphrodite."

"Cool your jets and we'll explain everything." Eros signaled for me with two fingers. "Serve us wine, Spiro, so we can drink to Ares and Eos."

"Eos?" His face turned red. "But I want Aphrodite, and she wants me!"

"Please, Ares." Eos batted her eyelids and parted her lips in the most 'come hither' way imaginable. "Sit here next to me, and we'll talk."

Grudgingly, Ares took his seat. "What's this all about?" The way he looked her up and down with undisguised animal lust in his eyes should have been insulting, but Eos ate it up.

"I'm *made* for you," she purred.

"You're made for *something* all right, and I'm imagining it right now." What a pig, charging at her with the hormonal equivalent of those made-for-penetration tusks that had done *me* in such a long time ago. She tittered, obviously flattered by his lewd attention, while I busied myself with the corkscrew and wine bottle. Hermes, in the meantime, started serving the soup.

"Ah, it's so nice to see you again, Nikkos," Ares said insincerely, with one eye glued to the steaming seafood chowder and the other on Eos, who had just adjusted her see-through blouse to draw attention to what was clearly visible underneath the sheer material. It seemed clear that he could care less about Nikkos. It was the food and one particular uninhibited woman that he was happy to see, *not* the waiter. "Give the chef my regards, please. His delicacies (and the one seated so close to him now that her barely-clothed body was literally pressed right against him) "always look so heavenly."

"I will sir," Hermes said, in that same baritone accent that he had practiced on me a moment earlier.

I poured the wine, starting with Ares, but before I could move on to the other two guests he had already downed his glass like it was a shot of whisky and was holding it up for more. The second serving suffered the same fate as the first, and it was not until I had re-filled him a third time to nearly overflowing that I was able to turn my attention to Eos and Eros.

Ares belched. "So back to business. I'll service you, sexy, if that's what you'd like, but then I'm moving on to Aphrodite. She decided against Adonis and wants *me* back instead."

"But Aphrodite lifted my curse! You know what *that* means Ares, don't you?"

94

He didn't answer her question, but instead glared suspiciously across the table at Eros. "Why would Aphrodite do that?"

I watched with interest, knowing that this conversational 'lead-in' was the equivalent of Cupid notching his figurative bow. "Because she's decided to unselfishly sacrifice her own happiness to make up her debt to Eos."

"What debt?"

"She ruined my life by making me into a perpetual slut," Eos commented without animosity. The 'tag-team' approach seemed to be working smoothly so far. "Sure, everyone wanted me for a one night stand; but beyond that?-forget it! It was fun for a while, but a girl gets tired of being the lead pony on a sexual merry-go-round after a century or two. I've been dying to settle down; and now that all those uncontrollable urges are a thing of the past, I can finally be happy-with *you*! Aphrodite is bowing out, and I absolutely *adore* her for it."

"That's ridiculous."

"Hardly." Eros was cool as a cucumber. "After what she did to Eos, Aphrodite feels that she *owes* her."

"Owes her *what*? That curse was a smoke-screen that gave Eos an excuse to openly be Eos. She was a floozy long before Aphrodite murmured the words and waved her magical hands over that nympho's infamous bedroom-mattress."

"That's not fair! I'm a changed woman now." Eos pushed her unrestrained breasts against the side of his arm and then placed her hand quite indiscreetly on his inner thigh, going in for the kill. "I love you, baby-I always have."

Ares responded to her advances like the cave-man that he was, taking her hand and leading it just a few inches further up his leg; but agreeing to another romp in the hay was *not* the same as assenting to a long-term commitment. He would definitely need that extra push; and that's when the bright red shaft of light, obviously representing some kind of strangely visible energy transfer, shot arrow-like from the center of Cupid's chest directly into Ares'.

"It actually looks like an arrow!" I blurted out, realizing in a panic that I had just spoken out loud; but it didn't seem to matter. Ares was staring now directly into Eos' eyes like he was hypnotized.

Hermes, suddenly himself again and no longer Nikkos, stood behind Eros. "He's been 'smitten', to coin a phrase." I touched my *own* face, confirming the familiar geography of my nose and chin, which prompted a hearty laugh from my mentor. "You're back to normal, too," Hermes assured me. "I must say, I'm glad of that. You're a much prettier sight than your homely counterpart; wouldn't you agree, Eos?"

She nodded, but didn't take her eyes off her man. She was obviously 'smitten' too, but her infatuation had been earned honestly. "How long will they stay like that?" I asked.

"For an hour or two," Eros replied. "His 'blood levels' will eventually taper off, but the durability of my love potion is guaranteed. Even though the glazed expression on his face will fade, his love for Eos will remain strong and unfailing for at least six centuries."

Hermes patted Eros on the back with congratulatory vigor. "Good show, old boy! You and Eos should be quite proud."

Eros wiped the fatigue from his face. "It always drains me a little, the whole 'arrow to and from the heart' thing." He sighed complacently, taking a drink from his untouched glass of wine and then raising it in Eos' honor. "But you deserve most of the credit, honey. Without your flirtatious assistance, my arrow would have *never* hit the mark." Eos, still oblivious to anything but her precious god of war, simply sighed contentedly.

"Here's to Eos and Ares," Hermes offered.

"*And* to Adonis and Aphrodite," Eros added. "May the four of you stay happy forever, living the dream!"

"Hear, hear," I chimed in. All it took was a few sips from my glass, and the room started to spin. Had my drink been spiked with some kind of gentle sleeping potion? No matter; because before I knew it, I was out cold.

Chapter 10
Rapid Eye Movement

Where in the world was I now? As I woke up from an unusually deep sleep, I looked around and tried to use my quickly petering powers of deduction to orient myself to yet *another* new location.

I was in a hotel room, lying on a bed facing a large picture window looking out on a mountain panorama that I didn't recognize. An open French door let in a fragrant breeze wafting in from scenery that could have come straight from *The Sound of Music*. I could be anywhere, really-the Swiss Alps, the Himalayas, or even the Canadian Rockies. I got up and walked outside onto the patio, contemplating the rocky terrain that extended downwards from my hotel room, ending abruptly 500 yards or so in what appeared to be a cliff-like drop-off that had been safely and tastefully incorporated into a railed-off observation platform.

I strolled out onto the slope, a few paces later turning to face the luxurious mountain chalet, which had ingeniously been built into the mountainside. Snow-capped peaks cradled the chateau on all three sides; and, as I craned my neck upward to scan the stone face of the mountain, I noticed a ski lift (or maybe an aerial tram?) leading from the base of the precipice into a narrow crag. The rope-like cables angled steeply skywards, eventually disappearing behind a jutting outcropping of granite half a kilometer or so above the lodge.

The air was crisp and thin, perfectly consistent with the high altitude. I retreated into the relative warmth of my room, closing the patio doors behind me and adjusting the thermostat to a more comfortable temperature. My luggage-two suitcases and a briefcase containing my laptop, notes and trip itinerary-had been stacked neatly in the corner next to the closet and dresser drawers. Someone (and I thought I knew who) had somehow managed to pack my things, check me out of my hotel in Polis, book and sign me into this high-altitude resort, and re-install my physical body and personal belongings *here*.

But where, exactly, *was* 'here'? "Okay, Hermes," I called out loudly, "I give up. Where am I?"

As usual, he startled me by abruptly materializing before I had even finished my sentence, his body stretched lazily across the bed from corner to corner, on his back with both hands behind his head.

"I've always loved this little getaway," he said. "In fact, I got lucky with Persephone once upon a time, here. That was *long* before she settled for Hades, of course, and in those days there was no hotel." He laughed. "If my memory serves me, I created a cozy little shepherd's cottage for our lovers' rendezvous." He sat up, walking to the picture window to take in the view. "Yep, this was the very spot, old boy. I'll never forget the gorgeous view-both lady *and* landscape, if you know what I mean." He winked. "I should really give her a call sometime. She's single again, I hear."

I waved away his irrelevant banter. "Where *are* we, Hermes? Forgive me, but I'm feeling a little bit like a traveling gypsy right now."

"Sorry for the sudden re-location, but you've been passed out for 12 hours or so. I slipped a little something into your drink so you could get some much-needed shut-eye. You certainly *look* refreshed. Are you feeling better?"

"In fact, I am. Now, please tell me where you've transported me, Hermes."

"I'll give you three guesses."

I sighed. "Switzerland."

"Now, now, Adonis. Let's be serious. We're still in Cyprus. The mountain behind us should be a dead giveaway."

I thought for a second or two. "Alright, I know. We're at the base of Mount Olympus."

"Exactly, Professor; and up at the top, you'll become acquainted very soon with the secret entryway to our new facility."

I nodded thoughtfully. "So, this is the so called 'Throne of Zeus'?"

"Yes, indeed, although technically there's really no throne."

"No throne," I mused. Now I was truly curious. "So what exactly *is* the set-up inside the home of the original twelve?"

"You'll see for yourself soon enough."

"I'm more than a little bit nervous about the hearing tomorrow."

"One thing at a time, old boy. You need to sign some papers first. We'll be taking care of that tonight, at dinner."

"Papers?"

"Yep. Contracts, pleadings, addendums, preliminary orders-I have them all right here." He patted a leather briefcase that had just materialized right next to him on the bed. "I wish I could convince Apollo to take this bloody job. Everyone seems to forget that I'm *not* the only deity with a law degree." He walked towards the door. "Dinner reservations are at 6 pm, sharp. Dress is business casual."

"Where?"

"Right here, in the hotel restaurant-under the name *Mercutio*, party of two. Oh, and bring your credit card. The client *always* pays when business is being served."

I shrugged. What was another hundred Euros or so, between friends? "No problem, as long as you remembered my wallet when you moved me here!"

He put out his hand, snapped his fingers, and produced my wallet out of thin air. I smiled. "I guess you're a magician, too. How many hats *do* you wear, Hermes?"

"Too many, I'm afraid. I'm planning an early retirement. One or two more years is all I need, according to my financial advisor. I'm almost there."

"Whatever I can do to help with that," I said sarcastically, as I took my wallet from his hand and slipped it in my back pocket. "Dinner's on me, then."

He nodded, smiled, and abruptly disappeared.

***

Just a few hours later, I waited patiently in the reception area of the hotel restaurant, called *Poseidon's Trident*. The greeter had handed me a menu to peruse while she seated a young couple, whose open affection with one another earned them a secluded table in the back section of the dining room.

I opened the leather bound booklet, finding several pages of mock parchment inside which cleverly announced the kitchen's offerings for the evening. *Ocean fare served at Neptune's table*, the witty aphorism declared. As I leafed through the culinary selections, I noticed that most of the choices were, in fact, seafood.

The young woman, who had returned from seating the newlyweds, flashed me a perfect smile. "Would you like to be seated now," she asked, "or would you rather sit at the bar and wait for the rest of your party to arrive?"

I looked at my watch, which said *5:45 pm*. "He should be here in ten or fifteen minutes, so why don't you seat me, and I'll have a drink while I wait for him."

She led me to a table by the window, which was set for two, just as Hermes had promised. I opened the wine list as I settled myself in my chair. "I'll have the house red, please," I decided; and a few moments later, a waiter brought me my drink. My watch now read *6:00 pm* sharp.

"Are you expecting your friend soon?" the waiter inquired.

If I knew Hermes, the waiter's question would provoke an immediate materialization, so with clairvoyant assuredness, I replied: "Here he is."

"Where?" The waiter looked around and behind, in a futile search for my dining companion. Seeing no one, he glared at me with a look that said, 'here we go again.' My guess is that he was all too familiar with the occasional bad joke at his expense.

"Right there." I gestured towards the chair across the small table from me, which was, predictably, no longer empty.

The waiter startled slightly at first, but then his astonished expression froze awkwardly on his face as Hermes waved his hand. "He'll be back in a moment," my friend explained with a smile; "and I assure you, he'll have a *much* different memory of my arrival when he returns!" Once again the performer, Hermes mimicked the waiter's new recollection of the last ten seconds. "'So glad you could make it, sir. May I take your coat and hat? Sophia, could you help this fine gentleman with these things while I get him a menu?'"

"He'll really remember it like that?"

"*Precisely* like that. He'll recall that I wandered in while the hostess was busy in the back." He snapped his fingers, and his hat and coat disappeared, presumably re-appearing on hooks and hangers in the coatroom. Hermes raised his empty glass in mock celebration. "This historic moment deserves a toast. Now I must wake our waiter."

He crossed his arms, nodded up and down once, and blinked his eyes in an exaggerated impersonation of a genie. The waiter instantly came to life. "We'll enjoy your best cabernet, Xenos," Hermes stated, reading the waiter's name-tag. "Do you have any suggestions?"

"Yes sir. I like the Mont Blanc. I promise, you won't be disappointed."

"1992 if you have it, old chap. It was a very good year." He winked at me. "It's quite pricey, but my client can afford it."

***

We drank a toast: to old friends, to new friends, and to various combinations involving this particular theme. Hermes, who apparently functioned as a toastmaster as well as Olympian attorney, drained two full glasses of the delightful Cabernet before his witty but long-winded cogitations had come to an end.

"Down to business," he declared as he pulled a surprisingly thick sheaf of papers from his leather briefcase. "Let's see, what shall we do first?" He thumbed through the stack of documents, pulling a paper-clipped section from the middle of the pile. "How about this one, for a start?"

"What is it?"

"A petition asking Zeus to void the 'Ares finds and kills Adonis and this time it's for real' arrangement."

"I'm all for that."

"Look at this attached document: exhibit A, mentioned in the second paragraph of page 2. It's Zeus' original decree, signed in blood and executed by big daddy himself, about two and a half millennia ago. These ancient documents fascinate me. When we're finished with all this, I think I'll talk to the curator of the Olympian Artifact Museum about purchasing them. I could make a fortune on this stuff."

"Signed in whose blood?"

"Ares', of course. He was literally seeing in red in those days, so it seems more than appropriate, wouldn't you say?"

"Sure, I guess." I took the pen that he handed me and signed the petition. "What's next, Counselor?"

"Patience, my boy." For the life of me, I still couldn't tell if his aristocratic accent, which sounded like Lawrence Olivier's theatrical interpretation of Hamlet, was natural or contrived. He pulled out another sheaf of papers, unclipped the stack, and pushed them across the table towards me. "Sign next to the *post its* on each page, and don't forget to initial each and every bottom right corner, immediately under the *mhe*'s."

"What's an *mhe*?"

"Mercutio Hermes, Esquire, of course-at your service, night and day, for only $350 an hour. That's my steeply discounted 'ancient friend' rate, of course." He took a sip of his wine, rubbing his eyes wearily with the other hand as he drank. "I think I need a vacation. All of this hard work is catching up to me."

The waiter came back, and we placed our orders. "Only a few more left here, Adonis. Let's get these done before the meal comes." He pulled out the thickest stack yet, pushing them across the table for me to sign.

"What are these?"

"Let's see. First, we have Aphrodite's affidavit confirming her celibacy for all these years. Second,

105

there's Ares' testimonial that his love interest is no longer Aphrodite, but Eos instead. Third, we have your verification that you are who you really claim to be. Fourth, there's the promise of fidelity between you and Aphrodite, and between Ares and Eos. Fifth, there's the disclaimer holding you harmless for any and all of the many mistakes you made as a mortal. And finally, here's our pleading, with the requested order attached, for you to be instated as a deity."

"So-six documents to sign?"

"In triplicate, with initials on each page as well. Quickly now, so we can enjoy our appetizers."

"Talk about rapid eye movement." My head started to spin as I gazed at one page after the other. "All of this legal mumbo-jumbo is giving me a headache."

"You don't have to actually read them; just sign, Adonis! You can trust me."

Fifty or so signatures and initials later, I finally finished. Hermes double-checked the documents, and with a nod of satisfaction he slipped them into his briefcase.

"Can I count on you to get me a favorable verdict tomorrow?"

"I'm absolutely and positively almost certain."

"That sure, huh?"

"Nearly so."

I sighed, deciding that continuing in this vein would only lead to a sleepless night. The meal was delicious, the bill no less than shocking, and my fatigue so surprisingly overwhelming that I fell asleep as soon as my head hit the pillow.

Chapter 11
Nocturnal Hallucinations

I faced the aerial tram with a significant amount of trepidation. I had never been good with heights, and if the steeply angled cable-wire gave an accurate reflection of the almost vertical pathway that soared into the rocky heights, my goose was cooked.

"You'll have to use the mortal entrance," Hermes had explained the night before over dinner, "since you're not initiated as a deity yet. I can't materialize you there, unfortunately. It's strict Olympian policy."

"I didn't know you guys *allowed* mortals into your secret clubhouse."

"We do, on occasion-like Hercules, Perseus, and Odysseus, just to name a few. Once there's a slain monster or two in the picture, induction into the Hall of Honor is almost a given, and attendance at the confirmation ceremony is mandatory."

"There's a Hall of Honor on Mount Olympus?"

"Oh yes, two doors down from the Olympian Artifact Museum. It's quite fascinating, actually, if you like that sort of thing. I strongly suggest that you check it out after your hearing. Just take the elevator to level 2, and follow the signs."

"Maybe another day. I think I'll be a tad bit preoccupied this time around. But back to my solo trip up the mountain-are you saying I'm on my own?"

"Just until you get inside. Once you enter the tunnel, a special discreetly-booked 'escort' will be waiting for you there."

"And who might that be?"

"Your one-and-only Aphrodite, of course!"

If she was the prize at the end of the journey, then I'd gladly take my chances. "Alright, then. Just tell me what to do."

"Take the tram to the top at exactly 5:30 AM, right before sunrise. After you exit, follow the mountain path to the left, which will lead you to the summit. Once you're there, look for the rocky projection that looks like a woman's profile-you can't miss it. Go around to the far side, and you'll see a symbol stuck to the stone face that looks like a lightning bolt superimposed on the planet Jupiter."

"Zeus' idea?"

He nodded. "Not very original, if you ask me. Nothing ever changes. Leave it to Pop to find any and every way to toot his own horn."

"How do I get in?"

"Place your hand on the symbol and it will recognize your palm print, revealing the hidden door. That's all you have to do."

"Easy enough," I had replied, then; but *now,* as I faced the dizzying aerial ascent, I couldn't help but think that I had spoken much, much too soon.

Since it was well before regular opening business hours, the loading platform was naturally deserted. I waited nervously for the car to arrive, which would undoubtedly be propelled by some sort of magic since there would be no cable car driver to steer the damned death trap this early in the morning. Finally I heard the rumble of my

108

approaching hearse, which screeched and rattled as it stopped on the embarking platform immediately in front of me, its door sliding open with a loud pneumatic hiss. Well, it was now or never, so I took the 'plunge', leaping across the rocking threshold into the bleak steel cage.

As the door slid shut behind me, I wondered what I had gotten myself into. I had landed shakily on a poorly maintained rusty metal platform, its ridged grid-work preventing me from skidding like an ice skater across the angled surface. I grabbed a nearby handrail to steady myself as the ancient cable car, circa 1950 or so, lurched around the corner to begin its creaking ascent up the mountain slope. As I closed my eyes, I realized that what I couldn't see might not hurt me. I started to relax-at least until the moment my ghost driver put the pedal to the floor.

The cab lunged forward, and the abrupt acceleration threw me to the floor, pressing me against the wall like an astronaut on the launching pad. The tram, guided by an unseen hand and propelled by some kind of supernatural rocket fuel, shot skyward like a missile. Although the car's hooking mechanism, attached God knows how to the cable line above, screeched and groaned as it slid along the tense wire, I seriously doubted that it actually served any useful purpose. I was trapped in a projectile that had a mind of its own, with the only consolation being that it reached the summit in less than a blink of an eye.

I scrambled frantically to my feet as I heard the door hiss open, afraid that if I didn't get out now I would be in for another deadly rollercoaster ride down the mountain and back up again. I dove frantically headfirst through the doorway, landing on a wooden receiving platform feeling grateful to be alive. "Thanks a lot, Hermes," I yelled. "If that was your idea of a practical joke, I'm not laughing."

I stood up, brushing myself off sheepishly and with as much dignity as I could possibly muster. Thank God there was no one around to see me. I stepped off the platform and onto a path lined by stones, my journey illuminated now by the first rays of sunrise, moving quickly upwards towards the rocky projection that Hermes had mentioned. I followed the path around the stony face, which did in fact look like the profile of a woman, until I finally reached the far side where I easily discovered Zeus' pulsing blue lightning bolt shimmering on the rocky surface, zigzagging on top of a glowing orange depiction of the planet Jupiter. I placed my palm lightly on the color-coded doorknob, and sure enough Zeus' logo gently disintegrated and a mahogany door with a brass latch and ornate hinges appeared in its place. A hand-written note had been hung carefully in the precise center, printed neatly on a piece of beige stationary with a black felt-tipped pen, and secured with perfectly cut square tags of scotch tape at each corner. *Limited access entryway*, it said. *Knock, please, before entering.*

I rolled my eyes. "Okay, Hermes, I'm knocking now." I rapped with two knuckles-no response; and then again-still nothing. After trying the door-handle and confirming my suspicion that it was indeed locked, I glanced again at the note, which was now entirely different. Hermes had re-written

110

his message, which now appeared in blue ink, on white stationary with black-edged borders.

Mortal entrance, I read. *Ring the doorbell, please, before entering.*

He had drawn an arrow underneath the word 'doorbell'. Following this visual clue, I discovered a glowing orange call button that hadn't been there a moment before. "I'm quite amused; now, would you please let me in already?" I pushed the buzzer as the note instructed and the door finally opened inward to reveal a smiling and professionally dressed Hermes, wearing a porter's hat and a short white jacket.

"Good evening, sir," he said, playing his role as well as any Hollywood actor. "May I take your coat?" He motioned me into a dimly lit foyer as the door closed behind me, the wooden entryway dissolving completely into the interior wall of the hallway as soon as the latch clicked shut. I handed him my sport jacket. "Enjoy your trip?"

"Very funny."

He held out his hand, palm up. "It's customary to tip your driver."

"In your dreams. If it's all the same to you, I won't be using the same car service on the way back down."

We stood at the far end of a long carpeted tunnel that inclined downwards into the depths of Olympus for 300 yards or so before dead-ending at an elevator. Behind me, the wall had re-constructed itself into wood paneling to match the hallway; and in place of the door, there now hung an oil painting depicting a pastoral scene populated with a flock of sheep tended by two shepherds. Stepping closer, I

111

peered closely at the picture, recognizing Hermes as one of the figures. The other was an adolescent posed supine with his eyes closed in a restful sleep. I looked over at Hermes for an explanation.

"That's my son Pan. The poor boy was always either falling asleep on the job, or pining over his unrequited love for Echo. Undoubtedly, he was dreaming about her in this scene." He winked at me. "Junior's fantasy never came true, but *yours* is just about to. Excited?"

"Nervous, mostly; which reminds me, I was promised a female escort. Where is she?"

"Patience, lover-boy. She's coming." He carried my tweed coat into a small alcove and hung it on one of the empty hooks. I was still studying the painting.

"I thought Pan was a goat, from the waist down."

"That depended largely on his mood at the time. Goat, horse, bull... " He shook his head. "That boy, with his distorted body image, has *never* been satisfied with his natural form. Thank the gods he's not mortal, because a cosmetic surgeon would have a field day with someone like him." He grinned. "My job as porter is done. See you in the courtroom, Adonis!"

That was all the warning I got, because suddenly he was gone. "Are you sending for Aphrodite now?" I called out.

"I'm right here," a voice directly behind me replied.

I turned, and she *was* right there, so beautiful that I literally felt as though my legs would give out on me. With my heart pounding in my ears and my breathing shallow, I thought *this is it; this is what it feels like to be head over heels in love*. "You are so very beautiful."

She smiled her beautiful smile and blinked twice; and as a result, she and I were no longer standing in the reception foyer.

Chapter 12
Groggy Proceedings

I was standing instead in a courtroom, right in front of an unoccupied judge's bench, definitely feeling like the accused on exhibit just waiting for his death sentence.

"Back here, Adonis." I turned around and saw Hermes motioning for me to join him at my reserved seat at the defendant's table. Behind him, on the opposite side of the railing that separated the audience from the legal action, Aphrodite sat with her shapely legs crossed in the front row, wearing a thigh-high black skirt, sexy open-strapped heels, and a low-cut sapphire-blue top that came very close to exposing too much. She would definitely have to change into something more appropriate for a wedding, if things today went my way.

"Where's Ares?" I whispered to Hermes as I sat down next to him. The prosecutor sat alone at the table to our right, behind a nameplate that read 'Palias Athena, District Attorney.'

"The Ares matter was settled in Chambers a few hours ago. All of our pleadings have been entered as orders of the court, except for the deity request. We'll have to argue for *that* one, and Athena over there will function as devil's advocate, as the Attorney for the State."

"Is the State really that diabolical?"

"It was just a manner of speaking, my boy. Athena's a tough cookie, but I think I've got her beat." The side door opened, and Hermes nudged me with his elbow. "I think we're ready to start."

The bailiff ('Themis', I read on her name-tag, which I found particularly ironic since she was the goddess of justice) stood and made the announcement. "All rise for 'the all-mighty', presiding."

"Is that Zeus?" He was clean-shaven wearing a pair of stylish bifocals and a long horsehair wig, dressed in a plain black judge's gown rather than a toga. "I thought he had a beard."

"He did, but he shaved it off last year. He looks much younger now."

"He doesn't look like a god. In fact, none of you do."

"What do you expect? Even the old timers have had to adjust somewhat to modern times. It just wouldn't do to have us all walking around in traditional garb, now would it? We'd be identified immediately as either who we really are, or as crackpots more likely. I, for one, would like to avoid scrutiny as much as possible. The publicity and those damn paparazzi can be absolutely brutal."

"What happens now?" I asked.

"Shhh."

"Attorney for the defense," Zeus said, in a surprisingly high-pitched voice, "how does your client plead?"

"Worthy of deity status, your honor."

"Is that a guilty, or a not guilty? Please clarify, Counsel."

"Well... *neither*, actually. All of the other charges have been dropped, and our pleadings have been signed into orders. Don't you remember, your Honor?"

"Careful, son-I'll charge you with contempt. Don't try my patience."

I looked at Hermes questioningly, and he leaned over to whisper behind the back of his hand. "It's early Alzheimer's disease, but he refuses to see a doctor." He cleared his throat. "Ah, not guilty then, your Honor. My client pleads not guilty to the charge of... whatever he is charged with."

Zeus nodded knowingly. "Yes, not guilty. And the State; what does the State charge, Athena?"

Athena stood up. "That Adonis is guilty of... not being very, um... godlike."

"Objection," Hermes interrupted.

"Overruled," Zeus said. "Let the State's attorney finish her argument, Hermes. Then you'll have your turn."

"Sorry," he said, turning to Athena. "Go on, Athena. I didn't mean to be rude."

"That's okay, you're forgiven."

"What's going on here?" I whispered. "Isn't she the opposition?" I felt more and more like Alice on trial in Wonderland.

"Common courtesy goes a long way here, Adonis. Just let me handle things."

Athena was speaking. "His parents were mortal, and he's lived countless mortal lives. It's time for him to die. He's had too many freebies already. Enough is enough."

"Is that all, Counselor?"

"Yes it is," she said with a decisive nod, and sat down.

"Now it's your turn, Hermes."

Hermes stood up. "Have a heart, Zeus. He may have had mortal parents, but his birth from the trunk of a myrrh tree is nothing short of miraculous. I'd even go so far as to say that his entry into this world was particularly deity-like!"

"Very convincing argument, Hermes; very convincing argument indeed. Go on, please."

"Two words: spousal privilege."

"Explain."

"He'll be marrying a goddess. She's a 'citizen' and he's a 'foreigner', but once they tie the knot he should *definitely* be given a permanent Visa."

"*Another* good argument, Hermes. I think you're winning so far. Do you have anything else to add?"

"Just give him what he deserves, Zeus. He's considered a deity already in some circles. Let's simply make it official."

Zeus' gavel came down hard on the bench. "Done. You're a deity now, Adonis. Welcome to the club!"

Aphrodite sprang up, ran around the barrier rail, and threw herself into my arms. "I love you darling."

"I love you too. Will you marry me?" What a ridiculous thing to ask-of *course* she would marry me; and in fact, she was suddenly wearing a long white wedding gown. Looking down at my shirt, I saw that somehow my street clothes had been replaced with formal wear, too.

"Yes I will Adonis. Let's do it now!"

Hermes took his place on my right as my best man, and Athena on Aphrodite's left as her Maid of Honor. "Do you, Adonis, take this beautiful goddess

117

of love to be your one and only partner and wife, now and forever?" asked Zeus, who was no longer sitting at the judge's bench but stood in front of us instead, in his role as Justice of the Peace.

"I most certainly do."

"And do you, Aphrodite, take this 'man-promoted-to-god', to be your lawfully wedded husband, from now until the end of time?"

"Yes, please."

"Then, with the powers vested in me by the Original Twelve, I now pronounce you man and wife. Adonis, you may now kiss the bride."

"Hold it," Hermes interrupted. "Aren't you forgetting something, your Honor?"

"I *never* forget anything!"

We all looked at each other, and an awkward silence followed. Hermes cleared his throat. "What about the ring?"

I thought I noticed Zeus' cheeks turn red. "Well, uh... yes, of course; so, did anyone remember to bring it?"

"It's right here." Hermes handed me a platinum band discreetly studded with a meandering line of brilliant diamonds. I had never seen anything quite like it.

"Do I have one too?" I asked, holding it delicately between two fingers.

"No. Traditionally speaking, a god *always* goes ring-less. Jewelry is strictly reserved for the fairer sex." I shrugged and slipped it on Aphrodite's finger; and just like that, she was mine.

"*Now* you can kiss the bride," Zeus declared; but I already was. The kiss was deep and long, and made me feel weak in the knees.

"Please be mine," she murmured.

"I *am* yours, now and forever."

Hermes shook my hand. "Good show, old boy; good show."

"Thanks for all your help, Hermes-you're a true friend." I turned to face Zeus. "And thank *you*, your Honor, for ruling in my favor."

"Don't even mention it," father and son both said in unison.

"So, what happens now, Aphrodite?" I couldn't wait to begin my life with the goddess of my dreams.

"You'll sleep, of course."

"Sleep? Why in the world would I sleep, at a time like this?"

"Because you're tired; and when you wake up, you'll know *exactly* what to do."

"But... " I protested.

"Hush," she interjected, stroking my head with her soothing touch and leading me down into a supine position on the courtroom floor, right in front of the judge's bench. "Sleep now, and awake to a new day."

Was it a spell she had cast on me? It must have been, for within seconds I was enveloped in the soundest slumber I could ever remember.

Chapter 13
A Recurring Dream

I awoke, groggy and disoriented, to Led Zeppelin's *Stairway to Heaven*. Was I still somewhere under Mount Olympus? Apparently not, I concluded, rolling over in my familiar New Haven apartment to shut off my radio alarm. The button pushed, I was greeted with unearthly silence and overwhelming confusion.

4:15 am, 3/12/15, my bedside clock stated in glowing green. This was the day I had been scheduled to leave on my trip to Cyprus, which I thought I had already lived through almost a week ago! "What's going on here?" I asked myself out loud, throwing the covers off and swinging my legs over the edge of the bed.

Had it all been a dream? Just a moment ago, it seemed, I had said my marriage vows in the depths of Mount Olympus, kissing my beautiful bride and wondering what my life with her would be like and when it would start. To the best of my recollection, I had drifted peacefully to sleep in front of Zeus' judicial bench because of Aphrodite's spell, after a multi-day whirlwind adventure that had seemed so intensely real. There *had* to be a way to prove that I hadn't imagined the entire thing-perhaps a token of love that I had received from her, or some other physical item that I could use now as confirmation that she really existed, and that my trip hadn't been a figment of my dreamer's imagination?

120

And then I suddenly remembered her letters. I rushed to the corner of the room where I had neatly stacked my packed luggage the night before, unzipping and unfastened all of the pockets and sleeves of both suitcases as well as my briefcase, searching frantically for one of the two notes that she had left me during my surreal adventure in Cyprus... but to no avail. I found no letters-just the emails from her that I had printed and carefully packed away the night before, intending to read them over again before we actually met.

Still unwilling to accept the truth, my mind raced through a number of implausible explanations, finally landing on the one that seemed to make the most sense. What if Aphrodite *had*, actually, sent me back in time, so that we could start over again, as husband and wife, in a more 'normal' and usual way? It seemed far-fetched, but so did the alternative-because let's face it, a dream never unfolds over a span of days, with every moment passing in real time like this one did. Well, if she and I were 'clearing the slate', I hoped and prayed that our agreements and contracts were still valid, because I certainly didn't relish the thought of watching her distract Ares again with a kiss and the press of her nude body against his, while I stood imprisoned and helpless in a massive piece of inert stone.

Well, there was nothing I could do about it now. *When you awake, you'll know what to do*, she had said to me in the courtroom; and she was right, I *did* know what to do. Although I had no clue what my future held, I did in fact know that if I didn't get moving, I'd miss my ride to the airport, and I desperately needed to catch that plane. Cytherea Agapo was my Aphrodite, real or imagined; and I would do everything humanly, *or* heavenly, possible to keep that reservation at *Taverna Hephaestus*, come Hades or high water.

The driver arrived promptly at 5:00; and by 8:30 I was seated comfortably in my first class seat. One of the stewardesses looked alarmingly familiar, and then I suddenly placed her. "Persephone?" I asked hopefully as she brushed passed me quickly during our preparations for take-off. She stopped, turning to meet my gaze with beautiful aquamarine eyes that seemed oddly devoid of recognition. Was she, or was she not, the same goddess that had handled my registration at the resort in Polis? Physically, she matched my memory of the hotel receptionist perfectly, right down to the tanned shoulders and the waist-length strawberry blonde hair. It simply *had* to be her. "Aren't you Persephone?" I asked again.

She looked me up and down, bending down and placing her hand on my arm when she had finished with her appraisal. "I'm Pamela," she said quietly, her lips close to my ear, "but I can be anyone you want me to be after we land." She straightened back up and winked. "Anything I can get you right now, sir, before our take-off?"

Now I couldn't help but wonder if I was, in fact, certifiably insane. What kind of mental illness manifested itself with such vivid and convincing hallucinations? One of my imagined dream-creations had not only materialized as flesh and blood, but she had actually flirted with me! I shook my head in disbelief, making myself a promise to see a psychiatrist as soon as I returned home from my trip.

I made my connection in London, and then in Athens; and an hour and a half later landed safely in Paphos. I rented my car, and as my navigator directed me just as it had before to my quaint hotel on the top of the cobblestoned hill, I couldn't believe my eyes.

"This is the exact same place!" I commented under my breath as I tipped the same porter, strolled through the same hotel lobby, and registered with the exact same front desk clerk. "This is unbelievable," I muttered, as I used the same card key to open the same door to the same hotel room. "It's *all* the same," I declared, feeling more than the usual run of the mill dejà vu as I unpacked my bags in just the same way as I had done a few days earlier-in my dream.

I napped; and, once again, the wake-up call gave me plenty of time for preparations before I once again found myself walking down the street. This time, though, I didn't bring a map. I knew exactly where to find *Taverna Hephaestus*, because after all I had been there before.

What would it feel like to actually see her, touch her, hold her, and kiss her-*whoever* she actually was? I rounded the corner and finally reached the restaurant, taking a deep and calming breath as I pushed open the door, finding myself face-to-face, as expected, with the same dark-haired maître-de that I had encountered before. This time, though, I knew exactly what to say. "Reservations for two, please. Look under the name 'Aphrodite'."

"Right this way, sir. She's already here." He led me politely to an occupied table located in the far corner of the dining room.

She was sitting with her back towards me, her dark walnut hair falling onto her smooth alabaster shoulders as she looked over the menu. She leaned slightly to the left, legs crossed to reveal her pleasing unforgettable calves and her smooth bare legs, wearing the same thigh-high black skirt, sexy open-strapped heels, and low-cut sapphire-blue top that I remembered from the courtroom yesterday. As I approached she turned, and our gazes locked. Her hazel eyes, which contained those indescribable flecks of emerald, mesmerized me just as much at that moment as they had on the night the night of our first encounter, on this same day last week-not here but in Aphrodite's Temple; and her full, inviting lips parted... in recognition?

"I think we've met before," I declared softly.

She smiled knowingly. "Yes, Adonis-we have."

I sat down in the empty seat across from her, taking her hand in mine and confirming with a smile that she was wearing a platinum wedding band, discreetly studded with a meandering line of brilliant diamonds. I could no longer say that I had 'never seen anything quite like it,' because of course I had.

"So what happens now, Aphrodite?"

"I think you know."

THE END

124

WITH TOWER AND TURRETS, CROWNED

*

This is a tale of witchcraft and passion that takes place in Dunyvaig Castle:

Lagavulin Bay, Island of Islay, Inner Hebrides, Scotland

January 31, A.D. 1143

Beginning at 2:00 AM and concluding at 7:00 AM

All night the witch sang,
And the castle grew up from the rock
With tower and turrets, crowned.
All night she sang,
And when fell the morning dew,
'Twas finished, round and round
Author unknown

Chapter 1
On the castle tower

As told by Rhian
2:00 AM

The night was cold and frigid, just like her. He had hoped that a baby would warm her heart; and soon, he would know if the bond of a child between them would soften her emotional hardness. His wife's labor, still in progress, had been long and difficult, and Rhian's frustrating vigil outside her bedroom chambers had left him feeling powerless and numb.

The mighty Rhian MacDhomhnuill, Gaelic warlord and Thane of Islay (a large coastal island at the southern limb of the Inner Hebrides of Scotland with sworn but tenuous allegiance to the Norwegian king) stood now on the balcony of his castle's soaring tower. Earlier, at mid-day, Rhian's wife, the Lady Sif, had been carried into her bedroom after collapsing in the banquet hall. Rhian, plagued with apprehension, had waited in the small antechamber outside her rooms for hours upon hours; and although his servants had done their best to make him comfortable, he became more and more concerned about the well-being of his child in her belly. After some time, the midwife came out announcing that Sif's water had broken, and that her contractions were coming more frequently. "All will be well," she said, but Rhian remained skeptical since the baby's arrival had not been anticipated for yet another month.

He had waited nervously, seated in a large chair by the fire as the hours passed, his nerves frayed by his wife's muted cries from behind closed doors. The platter on the table beside him overflowed with food, but it remained untouched. Unnerved by the uncertainty of the night's conclusion, he couldn't eat, drink or rest; to be honest, he couldn't even think. Finally, the heavy door to his wife's chambers opened, revealing an exhausted midwife whose gaze would not meet his.

"What is it, Bridget?" *Good news or bad, I need to know.*

"It will be soon now, my lord. The baby's crown is at my lady's entrance, and her pains are more frequent." Her demeanor was nervous and awkward, in keeping with a servant who is faced with the task of delivering an unsavory message.

"Go on, midwife. You are only the messenger. Say what you intend freely, without fear of reprisal."

She studied the carpet, rather than look at him directly. "She asks for you to take your leave, Master, so the sounds of her final efforts are made with some degree of modesty and privacy."

"Is that all?" Rhian frowned, annoyed at first; but then he shrugged. *If this is her wish, so be it.* "Go tend to her, Bridget, and assure her that I will not hear. I will go to my tower."

Secretly grateful, he and his shadow-a flickering and distorted shape on the torch-lit walls-navigated the maze of corridors, deserted at this time of night. He was tired, but sleep would not come easily until his child entered the world. He passed his bedchambers on the way to the spiraling staircase that led to his sanctuary in the highest tower of his castle: Dunyvaig.

Rhian began the trance-like ascent, his boot-clad footsteps echoing hypnotically in the dizzying cylinder of the tower stairwell. One hundred and ninety-nine steps later,

Rhian reached the small room at the tower's summit, where he was accustomed to spending many hours, especially of late, in private meditation. He stepped into the orange glow of firelight and warmed his hands in front of the hearth, where, on his direct order, a constantly replenished stack of wood blazed like a furnace, from nightfall until dawn, whenever the weather was cold. Plagued by insomnia of late, he was glad to have this warm refuge to visit on nights like this.

He took one of the candles from a recess in the wall, lighting the wick in the hearth fire and using it to flame the other dozen blocks of nearly frozen wax that shivered patiently in the icy stone. Orange lightened to yellow in the room, as the candlelight's illumination surged. He walked to his desk, where his journal lay open; sat for a moment, scribbling a few quick thoughts on the next empty page with feather quill and ink; and then got up, with a sigh, pushing open the double door that led him onto the small tower balcony. And this is where he now stood.

The freezing air of January's final day turned Rhian's warm breath into white mist, reminding him of the brevity of human existence since it was there one moment and gone the next. But the child that would soon enter his world would be, in contrast, a symbol of his personal immortality, in a way-conceived from his own flesh and blood and propelling his body's legacy beyond the boundaries of his own lifetime. A baby might also heal, in part, the regret that surrounded his arranged marriage to the heartless and stony Viking princess. His union with Sif in May just past had been an obligation of duress, conceived by Olaf the Red: King of Mann and the Isles, the Norwegian crown's local magistrate. Rhian's marriage was solely intended to strengthen political ties between the Gauls and the Vikings, which it apparently had; but by relenting to Olaf's scheme, Rhian had traded his happiness for pure misery. He sighed. Perhaps this son, or daughter, would fill the gaping emptiness.

Rhian's massive castle, Dunyvaig, was built atop the precipitous slope of a ragged sea cliff overlooking Lagavulin Bay. The full moon was a backdrop for drifting tendrils of grey clouds, which retreated from the blowing winter wind like defeated soldiers on an eerie lunar battlefield. The jutting terrace protruded precariously from the peak of the tower; and as Rhian stood on the edge of nothingness, he noticed a dark outline of a bird, perched on the stone railing to his left.

"Cadha, come." He used the name that he had given the resident osprey a few years before. Cadha meant 'from the steep place', which of course referenced her home on the highest castle turret. She had made the tower her permanent residence; and so far, she had tended to two separate sets of hatchlings during the past two seasons there, in a large nest that she had built on an exterior drainage

129

ledge, just five or six feet below the outer edge of the circular parapet.

She ignored his call, diving noiselessly from the railing and into the moonlit blackness below. Rhian laughed softly as he leaned out over the incomplete darkness that stretched endlessly on all sides of the tower's balcony, watching with happy envy as the beautiful bird of prey flaunted her glorious freedom. "Return soon, my friend," he whispered, wishing that he too could escape the prison of his castle, if only for a moment, and join her in happy flight.

The gentle, barely visible whitecaps of Lagavulin Bay were distant shimmering lines of undulating pallor, and his eyes saw them in a fleeting illusion as an army of brilliant white serpents that rode the waves in grotesque and orderly formation. He leaned forward over the battlement, bewitched and entranced by the optical illusion; and suddenly, the impact of the dizzying altitude hit him in a rush. Rhian stepped back from the ledge, nearly losing his balance before retreating with a pounding heart to safety against the stone wall right next to the open door that led back inside, startling severely when he felt the unexpected touch of a hand on his shoulder.

"Apologies, my liege."

Rhian turned towards the broad shadow standing right next to him, on the doorway's threshold. "You surprised me, Brenhin. I didn't hear you approaching."

He felt his friend and lieutenant's hesitation like a heavy weight. "I bring news of Lady Sif's labor."

If I must know, it should be now. "Well? Do you bring with you good news, or bad?"

"I bring you joy and sorrow both, my lord."

"Out with it, man! Am I a father, or not? A simple yes or no will suffice."

"You are indeed a father, Rhian. Your lady has delivered you a healthy baby girl, and she is indeed a beautiful sight!"

"Thanks to our God in Heaven," the thane whispered. "And my wife?" Perhaps Sif had died in the birthing-a terrible thought, he tried to convince himself.

"The Mistress of Dunyvaig is well, my lord." Brenhin hesitated, his voice hushed.

"If you have more to tell, then do so, my friend."

Brenhin looked down. "She bore you a second child, Rhian. It came as a surprise, shortly after the girl was delivered." He paused. "It was a stillborn son, my liege. The lady's cord was twisted like a noose around his neck."

Rhian fell to his knees. Sif had carried low and large, but no one would have ever guessed that twin babies had been growing in her pregnant womb, one of whom had been a potential heir and successor, whose unnatural demise may have very well been caused by the curse of his loveless marriage. *But I have a daughter*: healthy and beautiful, warmed now by the heat of her mother's bosom and the promise of a thankful father's arms. Rhian's heart surged with love and hope. This newborn daughter would be his special child, a beloved and radiant shaft of hope for the entire island kingdom.

Brenhin helped to him to his feet, a gentle hand on his elbow; and as he did so, a light flurry of snow started to fall softly on the balcony railing, like a blessing descending from the heavens. "Take me to my daughter, Brenhin. I will call her Aibhilin." Aibhilin meant *little bird*. The name came to him, at that very moment, as a natural choice, since the baby's coming into this world had coincided, like a premonition, with Cadha's appearance on his tower's railing.

Brenhin said nothing. *Is there more he is not telling?* Rhian looked carefully at his friend's expressionless face. *Yes, there is something more.* He grasped Brenhin firmly, with both hands on his shoulders. "Pray tell me what troubles you, comrade."

"You will see, Rhian, soon enough," he said, his voice soft and disquieting. "Come now, please." Brenhin turned away, walking brusquely into the tower room and heading purposefully towards the spiraling staircase. Rhian had no choice but to follow, so they descended, together, down the dark and seemingly endless stairwell.

Rhian had no idea what awaited him below; but whatever it was, he feared that it would change his life, forever.

Chapter 2
In Sif's sitting room

As told by Rhian
3:00 AM

Rhian followed Brenhin closely down the stairs, through the maze of corridors, and then finally into the antechamber of Sif's quarters. His lieutenant held the door open for his commander, but shut it behind him again as he took his leave so that Rhian could deal privately with his wife and her entourage.

Three attendants stood quietly in the shadowy periphery, their features shrouded in the sweeping drape of darkness that cloaked the edges and corners of the chamber, while their shadows danced grotesquely on the walls in the pulsing firelight, like macabre actors in some tragic performance. Bridget, the midwife, stood motionless in front of the fireplace; and in her arms, she held a child's body, concealed in a thin white blanket. *He is as still and cold as a piece of marble.* Rhian shuddered as the horrifying reality of the stillbirth started to hit home, but then he noticed that one of the servants standing in the shadows held a parcel that kicked with the joyful signs of life. *My daughter will be the happy antidote to this sorrow-but why in heaven's name is she out here rather than in there?* The child, by nature's order, should have still been in the bedchamber, suckling happily at her mother's breast; so why *wasn't* she? It was then, in a flash, that it hit him. Surely, this is what had troubled Brenhin so. *Sif does not want the girl!* There could be no other explanation for this unnatural separation of newborn from mother.

He would deal with Sif momentarily; but now he had other, more pressing issues to contend with. The thane approached Bridget, lifting the blanket that covered his son's ashen face. He was so tiny, so beautiful... and so sorrowfully lifeless. Rhian gently stroked the baby's cheek, which felt soft but cold, and the tears welled in his eyes, blurring his vision. *I can't bear this. I can't look, even a second longer.* He turned away abruptly, motioning to Bridget that he had seen enough so she bowed, covering the boy's face with the blanket, and turned to leave; but as she started to pass, Rhian laid a gentle hand on her arm to stop her. "My thanks, midwife, for your talents and knowledge. There was nothing you could do about the boy. I pray you should know this."

She dropped to her knees, stifling a sob, while one of the attendants stepped in to take the stillborn. Her eyes were red and bloodshot, and her cheeks were moist with grief. "You are kind and gracious, my lord. I am your true and faithful servant."

Rhian knelt down beside her. "I share your grief, woman, and I know your sorrow-because it is my own." He grasped her shoulders, helping her up; and while he was doing so, she locked his gaze.

"She does not want the girl, my thane." She whispered so no one else could hear. "I tried to give her the babe to nurse, but she pushed me away with such violence that I almost fell to the floor. She sent me out, demanding privacy and saying that I should never bring her daughter back or else suffer death as my punishment!"

He nodded grimly, knowing already that Sif had rejected her very own flesh and blood. "Worry not, Bridget. The Lady Sif mourns the boy-that is all, I'm sure. Perhaps with time... " His voice trailed off as he felt a secret panic deep inside, building like a brewing storm. In his heart, he knew the truth. *Time will not heal her troubled soul, and she will never love this baby.*

"Thank you, Master." She curtsied. "May God be with you... *and* with my lady." She turned and left the room accompanied by two of the remaining three servants, one of whom held his stillborn son. Rhian concluded that the last one, who stayed behind rocking his daughter in her arms, must be the wet nurse. Her features were obscured in the darkness of the room's corner, so he motioned her to step into the light. She did so, immediately causing Rhian to startle and look twice, his heart beating double-time in his chest.

"Can it be you?"

"It is, my lord."

As soon as the woman had stepped forward into the softly burning candlelight, Rhian recognized her immediately. Her dark auburn hair framed her strikingly beautiful face, dangling with a gentle touch onto her fair shoulders while her rich brown eyes searched his with tender boldness. "Oh my God," he uttered softly. "Is it really you?" He had never expected to see her again; and yet, here she was, standing before him like the dead, miraculously brought back to life. *My sweet Gwyneth-I have missed you so.*

135

Their relationship had ended abruptly, without a chance for either of them to even say goodbye. He often prayed for reconciliation, since neither of them had had proper closure; and now here she was, which meant that he would finally have a chance to make his long overdue amends. He had seen Gwyneth only once after their final autumn rendezvous, at the mid-summer banquet that was meant to celebrate Sif's arrival with her entourage from Iceland, two months after Rhian had bound himself to the frigid princess with spring wedding vows in a foreign land, with Olaf's threat the propelling incentive. Gwyneth had somehow been enlisted as one of the meal servers, attempting to cloak her true identity by lightening her hair and darkening her skin. Her eyes had given her away, though, as their gazes locked from across the room and his heart had filled with hope that they might enjoy a brief, secret reunion together, if even for just a minute or two after the festivities ended; but when the crowd dispersed she was nowhere to be found. She had gone, without a single word of explanation.

"Gwyneth." His voice cracked. "I thought I would never see you again." *Oh how lovesick I was for you then, and still am now.*

She bowed her head, and a tear ran down her cheek. "I am your humble servant, my lord," she said softly, with a curtsy.

He wiped away the tear, gently, with the back of his hand. "No, Gwyneth-I am not your lord. Rather, I am *your* servant, now and forever.*" They had, of course, never been social equals, but their intense passion for each other had somehow adjusted, or even reversed, this discrepancy. He had always felt consumed, somehow, by the ecstasy of their romance; and in their private moments, together, *she* had always been the one in control, not him. He would have done anything that she commanded; and at this moment he still felt the same way even though nearly a year and a half had passed since they had been together last.

"I have missed you, Rhian." Her eyes searched his for a reciprocal emotion, and he answered her without words. *The fire between us still burns hot.*

He held her face in his hands. "My life has been empty without you." He kissed her gently on the lips, and she closed her eyes. She was trembling. "Hush, my darling. All will be well." But would it? Having his ex-lover close by, in residence as his daughter's nurse maid, would be a very difficult situation to manage, indeed.

"I have prayed for this moment."

"As have I; but tell me, how have you arrived here in such an unlikely capacity?"

"I heard the Mistress of the castle was having a baby, so I inquired with her household whether a nursemaid might be needed. You see, I have been feeding my sister's baby these past two months in her absence, as an adoptive mother; and since my breasts are still engorged... " (she blushed) "...well, here I am."

He nodded, but her explanation raised more questions than answers. Surely she would have recognized the hazards involved in offering herself as a wet nurse to her former lover's baby, especially if she still had feelings for him, as he did for her. Not only did her presence risk emotional disaster for them both, but there was also real physical danger involved in having Gwyneth live under the same roof as Rhian's jealous wife. Sif was an utterly malicious woman who would never tolerate infidelity; and even if Rhian and Gwyneth never rekindled their physical relationship, the maiden's life would be in peril if Sif ever caught wind of their past history together.

Rhian lowered his voice. "You risk much by coming here."

"I know," she whispered, "but I had no choice. This, and much more, has been foretold, and we cannot change our destiny together."

"What mean you, Gwyneth, by 'foretold'?"

"A soothsayer showed me a vision of what will be, but I must be here, with you, for this future to come true."

"But Sif will have you killed if she finds out who you are!"

"She does not know me, Rhian. Just keep our secret and stay away from me, and all will be well."

"You are beautiful still, Gwyneth. I will not be able to stay away."

"Leave these thoughts, Rhian, and do not worry. I will seek you out when it is safe to do so, and when the time is right, very soon. I will handle this."

She was in control, as always. He thought back to that first night together two autumns past, when she had secretly joined him where he slept, in her father's barn. They had shared a kind of passion that he would never forget, and that he still longed for, especially now. Sif had rejected all of his advances since their wedding night, after they had lain

138

together in a single joining that had immediately made her pregnant; and ever since, she had insisted that they sleep in separate bedchambers. Sif claimed that the wellbeing of their baby demanded that she remain untouched for the entire duration of her term, but he knew better. She hadn't even tried to conceal her cold indifference to romance on that single night when they had had physical relations in the cold Nordic outpost of Iceland, where Sif had lingered for two full months in her family's castle before finally joining her new husband in Scotland. What a stark contrast between ice-queen and heated mistress, with the latter standing warmly beside him, virtually radiating passion. How he yearned for her to melt his heart again as she used to in days gone by.

"How is your father?" he asked. He remembered Donaidh's sincerity and kindness that day and night Rhian had spent recuperating after his injury, which had indirectly sparked the four-season long relationship between Rhian and the farmer's eldest daughter.

"He suffers from rheumatism, especially when the weather is cold as it has been this past fortnight; but otherwise, he remains in good health, and is still able to adequately manage his parcel of land."

Rhian thought back for a moment on the secretive circumstances surrounding his romance with the daughter of one of his island citizens. Gwyneth was a peasant and Rhian a powerful warlord; and although this class discrepancy became less and less important as their love for each other deepened, the unlikelihood of a legal union between a thane and a commoner imposed a cautious approach to their affair from the start. If they would never lie together legally as man and wife due to the social conventions of the day, he did not want to sabotage her chances to build a life with another man by flaunting their intimacy; so in order to protect Gwyneth's reputation, their covert trysts were known to no one-except for Brenhin. On many occasions, Rhian's loyal friend and lieutenant had escorted the cloaked and concealed damsel in the dead of night on horseback to arrive at Rhian's castle without being seen or recognized by anyone... or so Rhian had thought.

He laughed to himself at the irony. After a full year of frustrating vigilance, he had been on the verge of asking for her hand in marriage. Indeed, it would be a bold move for him to disregard the conventions of the day by marrying a woman of lowly birth, but truly, his thoroughly smitten heart had no choice in the matter. Quite simply, he had fallen deeply in love with her, and the pull was utterly irresistible. These carefully laid plans were thwarted, however, by the politics of royal ambition. Rhian had been called away abruptly by Olaf, the King of the Isles, meeting with him privately at his castle on Mann; and when Rhian returned to Islay, he grudgingly belonged to another woman. Humiliated and defeated, he could not face Gwyneth after being forced by Olaf into accepting the politically motivated pairing. Rhian sorely regretted the cowardly manner in which he had ended his relationship, by letter, with his one true love; but worse yet, Gwyneth had never known that he had fully intended to make her his wife.

Rhian recalled his fateful meeting with the self-serving Olaf, known disparagingly as Morsel to many in the island kingdom. The nickname referred to Olaf's shameless eagerness to exploit each and every opportunity to consolidate his power, no matter how small the morsel. The name also referred to his excessive frugality, which truly bordered on the obsessive, especially as it pertained to food. Rhian had heard that on one occasion, Morsel had actually had a servant executed for feeding some perfectly good leftovers to the cook's hounds.

Rhian had watched with curiosity from his seat at the other side of the table, as Morsel inspected a massive turkey drumstick that he held in his hand. Although he had already meticulously picked the last shred of meat from the bone, Olaf appeared to be searching for any remnants that might have escaped his thorough gastronomic attentions. Finally satisfied that it was truly devoid of edible flesh, he tossed the bone with contented nonchalance over his shoulder, reaching at the same moment for new quarry; but he was not prepared to attack his second helping just yet. Laying it on the table in front of him, he looked thoughtfully at Rhian as if he were appraising an opponent immediately prior to hand-to-hand combat. "I have promised my daughter Raignailt to the Thane of Kinn Tyre," he announced decisively, sounding as if he had just now made the decision and needed Rhian's approval before he could send out the wedding invitations. Rhian waited for the king to continue, but instead Morsel picked up the second drumstick and was now preoccupied with the task in hand.

Rhian frowned. It was out of character for Olaf to share any aspect of his personal life with his warlords; but even if he *had* been a friend or a confidante to the King of Mann and the Isles (which he certainly was not), Rhian could not believe that this seemingly irrelevant disclosure could be the reason for the private conference to which he had been urgently summoned and was now attending.

After a moment of silence, Rhian decided that Morsel would need some prompting to continue. "So your daughter will marry Somerled? This is an auspicious match, indeed."

The Viking, who was busy ripping the flesh from a turkey bone with his teeth, paused for a moment, raising his eyebrows as he glanced across the table at Rhian. "So you approve?"

Rhian knew Somerled, and respected him. A Gaul with a trickle of Viking blood in his veins, Somerled had proven himself in battle at Olaf's side, along with Rhian and a handful of other commanding soldiers. Both thanes were warrior prodigies in their early thirties who had gained the respect of the Viking king as well as the love of the people of the Isles, at an unprecedented early age. They had much more in common than shared political success, however. Equally handsome and good-natured, they both loathed conventional class distinctions and shared a love for the common people and the freedom of the open road-so much so that they would each, on occasion, enjoy disguised and protracted adventures in the countryside, during which they could secretly learn the true sentiments

142

and opinions of their own loyal subjects, or the citizens of neighboring islands and the mainland.

Shrugging, Rhian met Morsel's gaze with suspicion. "It matters not if I approve of the joining, my liege."

"Ah, but it does. You are a most powerful Gaul, not unlike your compatriot and friend. I would welcome your blessing, my loyal Thane of Islay, in this union between Gaul and Viking."

Rhian realized that perhaps Olaf had considered several matches for his daughter before deciding on Somerled, and that he himself had potentially been on the short list. He breathed a sigh of relief. Thinking of Gwyneth, he thanked sweet God in heaven that Somerled had been selected instead. Rhian smiled, nodding politely to Morsel from across the table. "I am honored that you seek my opinion, my lord. Somerled is the fortunate one in this engagement. Your daughter is beautiful, and the match will please this entire kingdom."

Morsel smiled deviously. "I am most happy to have your support. The blending of Gaul and Viking blood will make a new breed: strong, obstinate, and quite unwilling to bend to the will of a foreign master. You must participate directly in creating this new master race of islanders, Rhian, since you are already gifted with these most desirable character traits."

Rhian's mouth went dry. "Me?"

Olaf was now standing and his eyes were blazing with crazed intensity. "I will rule as a true king, as will my only child's children; but to do this, my plan must move forward without haste. You see, I have promised you to a Viking princess whose

143

beauty surpasses any woman in this kingdom, or any other."

Rhian couldn't breathe. "This cannot be," he managed to reply.

"But it is. The preparations for your nuptials two seasons hence, in Iceland, have already been made." Olaf leered at Rhian from across the table, the threat of enforcement clearly visible on his face. "Have you any thoughts on these arrangements, thane?"

Rhian took a deep breath to create self-composure, finally leaning forward in his chair, calmly defiant. "What if I refuse?"

Olaf laughed. "Yes, you may choose that road, but it would be a pity if anything should happen to that beautiful peasant mistress of yours."

Rhian felt dizzy. Somehow, Morsel knew about Gwyneth. "But, how... ?"

"My spies are everywhere. I know that she rides often, in the dead of night, with your lieutenant Brenhin, and that their destination is always Dunyvaig."

"Because she and Brenhin are lovers," Rhian blurted out, hoping against hope that Olaf had no further evidence to the contrary. "I have condoned their relationship."

Olaf shook his head, and Rhian's heart fell. "You can hide nothing from me. My sources know that she climbs naked into *your* bed when she arrives, *not* his. She is your lover, Rhian, and I will end her life if you refuse me."

The game was over. "I will do what you ask, if only you do not harm her."

144

"I knew you would come around. You are a wise man, and one who obviously recognizes the virtues of expediency." He smiled in smug satisfaction. "You will not be disappointed with the Princess Sif. Her beauty is legendary."

And so his fate had been sealed. Just as Olaf had promised, Sif's body was indeed exquisite (although he was only privy to the secrets under her discarded garments once); but Rhian soon found out that her soul, truly, was not. Now, he and Gwyneth would have that ugliness to contend with, if Sif ever discovered that the love of Rhian's life was actually one of the household servants.

Aibhilin's cries brought him back to reality. "She must be fed," Gwyneth stated as the baby rooted against her covered bosom.

"Sit here, my love, and tend to her." Yes, she *was* his love; and by some miracle of either coincidence or destiny, she was actually here with him, after so many long years of painful separation.

She did as he suggested, sitting down on the chair by the fire and cradling the crying baby in her arms, while at the same time loosening the interlacing string that secured the front of her nursing gown. She pulled the two halves of the bodice apart, pushing the fabric downward to unashamedly bare her engorged bosom, the nipples firm and visibly moist with cloudy beads of her mother's milk. Viewing her beauty thus exposed lit some dangerous fires within him. How could she be so nonchalant while he, in contrast, felt so desperate? "You have seen them before," she commented, obviously noticing his unwavering gaze.

"Yes, but so very long ago."

She pulled the baby towards her dutifully, attaching the suckling to one rigid nipple, which made the milk flow in a reflexive trickle from the other side as well onto the rounded fullness of her femininity. Rhian took a blanket from the back of the chair and placed it gently over her shoulders to cover the temptation. "What will you name her, Rhian?" she asked, as the child fed greedily from her bosom.

"I have decided to call her Aibhilin."

"'Little bird'? I like that name-very much."

Aibhilin nursed loudly from the other side now, and Gwyneth seemed relieved to have the building pressure reduced by the baby's feeding. A moment later she detached the child, who had fallen asleep in the middle of her first breakfast. "My dear Rhian, she is beautiful. I wish she was our child."

With a pang of regret that he knew she shared, he softly touched her hand. Words were not necessary since the bitter tears trickling down his cheek spoke instead. He smoothed his hand over his newborn daughter's fragile head as she nursed. "I love you, Aibhilin;" *and I love you, Gwyneth.* "Welcome to this world, my precious child. I am your father, and we will know each other well, I pray."

"She is her father's daughter. Look at her eyes."

True, her eyes were blue, just like his, and her hair just as fair. He gripped Gwyneth's hand tightly. "Yes, she is a special child-a kind and generous gift from God. I will treasure her, and I know she will change my life." Rhian gently took the dozing

146

infant from Gwyneth and cradled her in his own arms, holding her tightly against his chest and rubbing her back with a fatherly caress. Gwyneth in the meantime lifted her gown to cover her breasts; and rising to her feet, she touched Rhian's hands lightly as he held the newborn.

"You will be good to her, Rhian-kind and tender, as you always were to me." She was crying now, and he wiped the tears from her eyes, causing her to reach up and hold the back of his head with both hands. She kissed him, just as he had done to her a few moments before, but it was all too brief, by necessity.

"We can't do this, my love. Someone will see us... "-*like Sif.*

She nodded her agreement, disengaging the embrace and stepping back from him with a sigh. "Bring Aibhilin to her now, Rhian. Perhaps you will be able to convince her to accept her child, where others so far have failed."

From the corner of his eye, he saw a black shape jump from the chair by the fire. It was Freya, Sif's cat: his wife's 'familiar', brought with her from Iceland. The unholy animal was never far from her mistress; and as she crossed the room directly in front of Rhian, the castle's master shuddered. The pitch-black feline's emerald eyes peered through cunning slits as she settled on her haunches outside the bedroom door, waiting for Rhian to let her in. "You are right, Gwyneth. I must try... "-*although the price to enter that bedroom may very well be my soul.*

With silent resolve, he crossed the room and placed his hand on the cold iron door handle, steeling his nerves for God knows what, waiting for him on the other side of the threshold. Freya slipped through first as soon as he cracked the door open, disappearing into Hell's mouth with quiet enthusiasm, which Rhian hardly shared. A moment later he apprehensively followed his tainted escort inside into a darkness that he was more than a little bit surprised to discover was considerably less black than it was red.

Chapter 3
In Sif's sitting room

As told by Gwyneth
4:00 AM

Gwyneth watched nervously as Rhian disappeared into his wife's bedchamber and closed the door behind him. *If only I could walk by his side, grasping his hand tightly to help him face her.* She knew, however, in her heart of hearts that he would emerge eventually from a failed endeavor, Aibhilin still clutched to his broad chest and his face painted with disappointment.

Gwyneth knew what Sif was, because the fortune-teller had shown her. All of the rumors circulating now throughout the kingdom about the thane's wife being a black sorceress were actually true, but Gwyneth had known it even before the talk began-not only because the soothsayer, Ealasaid, had warned her, but because of what had happened at the wedding banquet last summer.

Gwyneth had changed her appearance so that she could attend the party as a server and not be recognized by Rhian, using lemon juice and white vinegar to bleach her auburn hair blonde, and wolf-berry extract to darken her smooth fair skin. After flattening her buxom chest with a tightly drawn corset, she had also padded her slim hips with the bulge of a feather-filled waistband. She stayed far away from Rhian; but despite this precaution *and* her disguise, she could tell when their gazes locked that he had quickly unmasked her.

As had Sif, it seemed-although it wasn't recognition but random selection that had guided the interaction. The new Mistress of Dunyvaig sat in close physical proximity to her new husband, immediately to his right, but did not engage in conversation with him, or anyone else at the royal table. *She is beautiful*, Gwyneth remembered thinking at the time, *but she seems colder than the icy land of her birth*. The red-haired devil seemed to be sizing-up each guest, servant, and dignitary alike; and momentarily, her steel-blue gaze found Gwyneth's and gripped it in a terrifying supernatural stranglehold, reaching across the room with uncanny paranormal strength. Gwyneth had literally felt the oxygen being sucked out of her lungs, remotely, by some kind of visual enchantment-impossible, most would say, yet it was happening to her, and in a moment she would surely be dead if the sorceress did not let go. She gripped the edge of a table, steadying herself while the room started to spin; but then it was over, just as quickly as it had started, simply because the witch had looked away, moving on to another victim... *like Rhian*. Gwyneth knew at that moment that her ex-lover was in mortal danger; and she vowed, as she tossed her apron in the corner and fled out of the castle and to the safety of the countryside, that she would come back soon and rescue him from the demon disguised as his beautiful new bride.

The very next day she went to visit Ealasaid, carrying a basket of eggs to use for payment. The old woman, blessed with the gift of future-seeing, took the gift from Gwyneth with muttered thanks and a nod, placing them carefully on the shelf next to countless bottles and jars of herbs and remedies.

"What brings you here, child?" The 'seer' had already gathered two or three bottles that were not marked, sifting a small amount of each powder into a large ceramic bowl, before she had even asked the question.

Gwyneth laughed. "You already know why I'm here, Ealasaid. Why else would you be preparing the looking-bowl?"

Ealasaid smile was toothless. "Yes, I know why you come here." She poured some water from a heavy jug on the counter into the bowl; and, after mixing the contents with a swirling motion, the old woman carried her seeing-potion over to the table, laying it carefully in front of Gwyneth. "You seek the future's vision, and with it my counsel. Is this true, Gwyneth daughter of Donaidh?"

"Yes. I need to know about Rhian."

"Indeed; but he is not in your thoughts unaccompanied. You also seek the truth about his lady."

"Yes. I fear he is in danger."

"My looking-bowl will tell us. Rest your fingers in the seeing-water, child. The potion will draw your future into the liquid, and I will tell you what is reflected in the magic pond."

Gwyneth did what Ealasaid asked. The water was tepid; but despite its warmth, Gwyneth's fingertips felt icy and numb after a few moments, and her hands began to tremble. Suddenly, she felt a chilling surge of energy travel from her hands into her shoulders and back again, causing her to gasp with alarm. She started to withdraw her hands as a natural reflex, but Ealasaid grasped her wrists to stop her. "The bowl has made contact with your future. Be still and the chill will pass. Let me read your future now, lass." Gwyneth relaxed; and just as Ealasaid had promised, the uncomfortable sensation in her fingers, hands and arms gradually subsided.

Ealasaid looked into the water, passing her hands over the surface of the liquid to draw the images from Gwyneth's psyche and into the depths of the bowl. Gwyneth studied Ealasaid's face, which had become flat and expressionless. Her eyes stared trance-like into the calm surface of the potion, intensely engaged in their task of observation and interpretation. Finally, she spoke. "I see two children. The first is your sister's child, and the second belongs to your thane. You will care for them both."

"But my sister has taken no lovers!" Or had she? Now that the thought had been planted, Gwyneth suddenly realized that Caitie had gained some weight of late, mostly centered in her belly.

"She is with child, conceived when the winter snows had newly melted into an early spring, after her first and only encounter with a wandering minstrel." Gwyneth nodded, remembering that first day of March when a most handsome singer had stopped to perform in the village square. "Your sister will abandon her boy right after his birth two seasons hence, leaving him in your protection while she searches in vain for the traveling father. You will nurse the child and produce copious milk so you will be able to nourish your thane's girl as well."

Gwyneth's mouth felt dry. "Is this truly *my* destiny you read, Ealasaid?"

"The bowl has drawn your future from your very own digits, lass. What I see will come to pass, as sure as the day is long." Ealasaid looked deeper into the water, which seemed to ripple with subtle movement around each of Gwyneth's submerged fingertips. "Beware of the girl's mother, who has hair the color of burnt copper and a heart as dark as night. She has the soul of a black sorceress, but her daughter is pure and bright. The baby is truly her father's child." Ealasaid's eyes moved over the surface of the water and then rolled behind her eyelids. "The thane and his unborn child are both in danger. You will be their salvation, should you choose this road."

"How, Ealasaid; tell me how!"

"Go to the castle on the eve of the Lady's early labor, on the final day of January. They will need a wet nurse, and you are the one they will choose."

Gwyneth pulled her fingers from the water abruptly, accidentally overturning the bowl as she did so and disrupting Ealasaid's trance. "Calm yourself, child." The seer reached for a rag to dry the spillage. "You must be cautious in this endeavor, for there is danger mixed with happiness in these prophesies."

Gwyneth pushed away her chair, unconcerned with the old woman's warnings, reaching across the table and warmly grasping Ealasaid's hands in thanks. "You have just made me the happiest lass in all of Islay. If what you say is true, I will be reunited soon with my sweet Rhian."

"You will be with him again, for better or for worse-this much is certain; but there is more. The Lady of Islay you may very well become, unless the witch finds you first."

"Can this be so?"

"It may come to pass; but the truth has two sides, my child. Just like a coin tossed in the air, the outcome of either up or down depends much on the prevailing wind. Be not rash, Gwyneth-caution must precede passion."

She threw her arms around Ealasaid's neck, kissing her tenderly on the cheek while her heart beat wildly in her throat. Grabbing her shift, she dashed excitedly out of the hut, while behind her through the open door she was pursued by Ealasaid's final call of warning. "Let your heart guide you, lass, but hear also the whispering voice of reason. I fear for you, child...that, I do."

***

The next day, as Gwyneth and her sister fed the goats and sheep together after their evening meal, Caitie shared a secret that Gwyneth had entirely expected her to tell. "God in heaven sent me a bountiful gift, a few months past," she revealed, her voice low and her eyes skittishly furtive.

"And what, pray tell, might that be?" Gwyneth pretended no foreknowledge of the answer.

"Do you remember the singer who arrived in the village to perform on that warm day in March?"

"Of course I do." Gwyneth leaned across the grain bin and spoke in a whisper. "He was exceptionally tall, dark and handsome."

154

"He was *beautiful* sister, and he actually took a fancy to me-can you imagine?"

"What happened?" Gwyneth tried to feign ignorance, knowing full well that the minstrel's seed had been planted in Caetie's fertile womb that spring-like day, and that his baby was nearly half-term at this very moment in her barely swelling belly.

"I stopped for a moment to listen to the music he was playing on my way home from the market, and when he had finished he started to load his packhorse so I approached him, simply to give him a moment of good cheer." She sighed, and a dreamy look came over her face. "He had just fastened the final binding on to his satchel, looking at me with mischief in his eye and his arm muscles bulging. I couldn't resist him, sister. The pull was simply too strong."

"You didn't *seduce* him, did you?"

"Please do not judge me! I have never seen a fairer face, or a brighter smile."

"It is nature's way, sister, and we are not meant to resist. Tell me, now-what happened next?"

"I asked him if he had a spot to rest. 'Alas, no, beautiful maiden,' he answered me in a deep and irresistible voice. 'There are none, here, willing to offer a traveling stranger shelter. But no matter, it's unusually warm and clear for this time of year. My horse and I will find a tree to rest under together, between this village and the next.'"

"So how did you answer?"

"I said there were thieves in these parts, who might take his belongings, or even threaten his life." She smiled naughtily. "He believed me, and asked if

I knew of a place where he could spend the night in safety."

"You might have offered our barn. You know father is the hospitable sort." Gwyneth thought back to that autumn night when *she* had seduced a traveler in disguise while he lay asleep on the hay.

"I had a more *private* spot in mind. I told him of our secret clearing in the woods, and then I led him down the overgrown path to our secluded spot."

"You were bold! You are not usually so forthcoming, sister!"

"Something came over me."

"It was surely fate's hand that placed this blessing on you." And now that same hand would lead Gwyneth back to Rhian. "Was he gentle, sister?"

"Oh yes, it was perfect. I have found my true love, and there will never be another." She looked down, concern sweeping over her face as she touched her stomach gently. "I fear my indiscretion has gifted me with a different kind of blessing, though."

Gwyneth took her sister's hand. "I only just noticed, dear Caetie; but worry not. I will help you with your minstrel's special present, as will mother and father, I trust."

Caetie threw her arms around Gwyneth's neck, kissing her cheek repeatedly. "I will pay you back in kind, when you give birth someday to your own son or daughter."

So it was that Caetie grew larger and larger as the months passed; and as her nine month term approached in late November, her sadness deepened.

"I must find him, Gwyneth. I *know* he loves me."

Gwyneth, having some knowledge of the future from Ealasaid's glimpse into the seeing bowl, knew that Caetie would leave as soon as her son was born; but she knew nothing of the ultimate success, or failure, of her sister's quest. "I know you love him," she said; "and I know that you must search for him."

"Will you help me?"

"Yes, by caring for your son with my own body's warmth and an adoptive mother's milk."

And so it happened just as the soothsayer predicted. Caetie's labor was brief, and her son, whom she named Seoc, was strong and healthy. She gave him to Gwyneth, whose breasts engorged quickly in response to her nephew's persistent suckling; and just two days later, Caetie packed a small satchel and said her goodbyes.

"Travel safely, sister... and Godspeed."

"Take care of Seoc."

"I will, Caetie."

And she did, until Caetie returned just two months later-frozen, exhausted, forlorn, and alone. Her first of many searches for the father of her child had been tragically unsuccessful.

***

Gwyneth had fallen asleep on the chair in the sitting room, waiting for Rhian. She awoke with a jolt to find that he was standing next to her, with Aibhilin clutched tightly to his chest and a hand on Gwyneth's arm. He looked visibly shaken-his face

157

ashen, and his lips trembling. She searched his eyes to ask the question, and he responded with a simple shake of his head. He had failed, just as she had predicted.

She rose to her feet, noticing at the same time a moist, bloody gash extending across the back of Rhian's left hand, partially covered with a hand towel. "What happened?" she asked calmly, taking charge as she usually did, wrapping his wound tightly and tying the bandage to stifle the bleeding.

"I have learned a terrible truth about my wife," he responded. "I fear this infant, after all, will be motherless."

Gwyneth squeezed his uninjured hand lovingly and transferred the sleeping Aibhilin without waking her from his arms into hers. "No, Rhian, a mother she shall have, may God be my witness!" She kissed the child tenderly on her cheek; and with new resolve, Gwyneth retired with her baby to the nursery quarters.

Chapter 4
In Sif's bedchamber

As told by Rhian
4:00 AM

Rhian entered his wife's bedchamber with Aibhilin clasped in both arms, the memory of Gwyneth's tender kisses from a few moments before giving him strength. Could their love be rekindled, even as he struggled with the complications of this cursed arranged marriage and the tragedy of a heart-breaking miscarriage? Despite the seemingly insurmountable barriers, he felt a glimmer of hope in his demoralized heart.

The room was bathed in an eerie blood-red light, which made him stop dead in his tracks. He re-adjusted Aibhilin into the crook of one arm to free up the other, stepping cautiously towards a scene that looked familiar, at least in his mind's eye. Was this what Brenhin had seen when he went to Iceland as Rhian's emissary two years past? If Rhian had had any doubts about his lieutenant's story, his skepticism had now turned to rage and fear.

Sif sat cross-legged and naked, her head bowed in intense concentration as she stared intently into a glowing orb made from some sort of crystal, completely mesmerized by what she appeared to be viewing inside. Her smoky burgundy hair spilled wildly onto her shoulders and breasts, its redness enhanced by a crimson aura of light, produced by the globe, which literally drowned the pale beauty of Sif's nudity in the color of blood. After a moment or two she brought the glass close against her body while leaning back against her pillow, touching it onto her skin with a tenderness that made the object seem almost human. It was an odd and provocative scene that Rhian knew he was not meant to see (nor Brenhin, when he had stumbled upon the identical ritual); yet here he stood: an accidental voyeur whose husbandly rights of contact had been denied and apparently given to an inanimate other.

Rhian now had an unobstructed view of Sif's exposed introitus, which showed no evidence whatsoever of the traumatic labor that she had just experienced. Her labia should have been swollen and torn, but instead they looked smooth and untouched-virginal, in fact. Had the object that she held so close now to her birthing place healed her? Perhaps it emanated *energy* as well as light, repairing the damage her sex had sustained during childbirth with unbelievable and unearthly rapidity? It was a strange thought, but one that his intuition guessed was correct.

Be very careful, Rhian. God (or the devil, more likely) has given the orb's radiance unearthly power, just as Brenhin had warned! The people of Islay, *and* Rhian's first lieutenant, claimed that Sif practiced witchcraft. Her dark maroon hair and unusually reserved demeanor were fuel for wild speculation that the thane's new wife had access to the supernatural; and now, looking on the globe and Sif's unnatural mental and physical preoccupation with it, Rhian was inclined to think that they were indeed correct.

160

Sif's mother, Brynja, had raised her daughter on an icy but sprawling estate on the frigid coast of distant Iceland, which had recently been settled by Norway's semi-exiled royalty. Brynja had been the beautiful mistress of the murdered Norwegian king Harald Gille, and Sif was his bastard daughter. Mother and daughter lived together in a remote castle on the Nordic outpost, where they were provided every luxury, by order of the Norwegian court-wanting for nothing, by anyone's standards, whereas in reality, both Sif and her mother were prisoners in their own luxurious mansion.

Sif's union with Rhian, which had been arranged by Olaf, the Viking Lord of Mann and the Isles, seemed to benefit all parties involved. Inge Haraldsson had been made child-king when his father Harald Gille had been slain; and Sif, his half-sister, now a beautiful young woman, naturally posed a threat to his throne. She was an awkward thorn in Norway's side, so marrying her to a foreign warlord in a far-off Viking territory in Scotland would finally neutralize a potentially volatile situation. Sif's engagement and eventual marriage to Rhian was a welcome relief to her mother, as well. With the threat to Inge removed, Brynja's banishment from her beloved Norway might finally be lifted.

Olaf had his own agenda, of course, with the blending of Gaul and Viking leading to consolidation of his own power as his sole objective; and Brenhin, as Rhian's closest confidante, had been none too pleased with the arrangement. Shaking his head at the time, he had warned Rhian that a marriage designed by others would end in tragedy, and possibly even violence, for everyone involved. "Rhian," he had implored, "your heart belongs to another! Do not do this to yourself, to Gwyneth, and to the people who love you so dearly. Bow not to Olaf's selfish whim, my friend."

Rhian shook his head. "There is much you do not know. I must marry this Viking princess, or else many in our island kingdom will suffer the dire consequences. Do not press me on this, my friend."

Brenhin touched Rhian's sleeve and leaned forward in a gesture of secrecy. "There are rumors about the Viking girl, my liege. Although beautiful, they say that she has been unable, or perhaps unwilling, to attract desirable suitors. Despite her fiery beauty, she is aloof and detached. Some even say that she is a witch!"

Rhian had laughed nervously. "Surely you do not believe such tales, Brenhin. Sif has been raised in exile, and any stories about her have surely been fabricated by her enemies."

"I am simply repeating what I have heard. I fear that this match will be ill-fated. Mark my words."

"I have no choice, Brenhin." Rhian clenched his teeth. "Morsel is most powerful, and his might is reinforced by the crushing strength of Norway's army. If I defy him, we will be overrun and defeated in the blink of an eye. And then, there's Gwyneth's safety to consider."

"Gwyneth?"

"Olaf knows about her, and has threatened to kill her if I do not agree to this union. That's why I have no choice, and must marry Sif."

162

The defiance painted on Brenhin's face instantly transformed into resignation. "What have you told her?"

Rhian had looked down, ashamed, and couldn't meet his friend's gaze. "I could not bear to tell her in person. I sent a messenger with a letter, explaining that my duty requires this sacrifice of me, but that I will always love her, with my whole heart and soul."

Brenhin seemed to accept this, although Rhian knew that his friend did not condone the impersonal approach his thane had chosen to end the once in a lifetime relationship. He sighed. "How can I serve you now, Rhian?"

"Go to the Nordic outpost, even though the winter winds will soon blow strong. This cursed marriage must be sealed with signings and exchange of treasures, which you shall accomplish, while at the same time observing my intended. In your welcoming capacity you shall also function as my eyes and ears. When you return to fetch me for my wedding this spring, after the Arctic blasts have subsided, you will tell me all that you have gleaned."

"I am at your service, my lord, and will leave first thing in the morning with my most trusted men." And so, as Rhian stood at his wife's bedside watching the orb communicate with her via contact against her flushed and moistened skin, he recalled with a chill of fear his lieutenant's recounting of his trip to Iceland.

"The castle was like a frozen extension of the Nordic coastline," Brenhin told Rhian after his return; "and on the day of our arrival, we were

163

welcomed into the warm castle by Sif's mother Brynja, who also hosted a sumptuous banquet that night. Sif was glaringly absent from the festivities."

"Absent?"

"Yes. Brynja apologized profusely, promising that we would meet the Princess on the morrow; but when the next day had come and gone, there was still no sign of her."

"Surely you saw her, if even briefly, during your lengthy stay!"

"I did, my liege, but it was quite by accident."

"Explain."

"The night before our departure, I tossed and turned restlessly in my bed, worried that I would return from my mission without succeeding in the most important of my varied assignments. Finally, I rose in the dead of night, deciding that a walk through the deserted halls of the castle might help to clear my mind. A few minutes into my sojourn, I approached the end of the main corridor and heard a woman's voice coming from the end of a small alcove located to my left. I turned the corner and found myself in a short hallway that led to an ornate mahogany door, behind which the vocal tenor had become decidedly agitated. Thinking that a damsel might be in need of assistance, I pushed open the door without hesitating, fully intending to be faced with a maiden being accosted by a rapist or worse."

"So what did you find?"

"I was standing in a fashionably decorated sitting room that adjoined a lady's bedchamber, which was illuminated in a moist unnatural way by a blood-red fluorescence streaming through a partially opened separating door. My curiosity

164

piqued, I hid myself quietly in the corner between the wall and the doorframe, and what I saw when I peered cautiously around the edge of the doorjamb both troubled and alarmed me."

"Was it Sif?"

"Indeed it was. I had no idea that I had rushed into the Princess's bedchamber, or that her physical appearance would be so compelling. She was naked, sitting cross-legged on her bed with a glowing orb held in the cup of her outstretched palms, with which she was engrossed in a one-way conversation that resembled a demon's incantation, spoken in a language that I could not recognize. The crystal sphere produced a bloody aura that consumed her, making her entirely oblivious to my observer's presence. She was engaged in a mental communication with her instrument that soon became physical."

"How so?"

"She leaned back onto her pillow and pressed the object onto her skin with a tenderness usually reserved for a lover."

Rhian signaled 'stop' with a raised hand. "I have no desire to hear of such things."

"But you must. The object was most unholy, and Sif was either its mistress or its slave-I could not tell which. Knowing full well that if I was discovered spying on such a moment that I would probably be thrown into the castle's dungeon or run through by one of the royal guards, I withdrew immediately."

So here Rhian stood, finding himself in an oddly similar position, wondering if he should follow Brenhin's lead from last winter and escape before Sif noticed him, or confront her. Being the brave soldier that he was, retreat was not in his nature, so he braced himself with one knee resting on the edge of the mattress, clutching the sleeping Aibhilin tightly in one arm while reaching out with his other, intending to touch the object and perhaps remove it from Sif's grasp, and in so doing break the evil hold it had on her. *She will either thank me for it or curse me*, he thought as he began to execute his plan; and that's when he felt a ripping pain on the back of his hand.

He drew back with a jerk, shocked to discover a long gash extending diagonally from his knuckles to the base of his thumb at the wrist. It was already gushing blood, so he grabbed a hand-towel folded neatly at the bedside and did his best, one-handed, to tamponade his injury. Had empty air inflicted his injury? It seemed so, at first, but then he saw the cat, sitting calmly on her haunches licking a blood-stained paw, strategically placed between Rhian and her owner in the exact spot where his hand had encountered a decidedly invisible assailant just a few seconds before. Had the witch's 'familiar' been cloaked and then uncloaked by some demon's trick, engendered by the orb or more likely by its mistress? A shiver of fear passed through him as he started to back away, convinced now that he needed to escape before Sif awoke.

His wife was still entranced, lost in some sort of supernatural communication with her globe, her lips moving in whispered incantation answered silently by glowing red touching on her skin, just as Brenhin had described. Her uttered spell would find him if he didn't hurry, so he moved quickly but

166

quietly back to the door, opening and closing it without a sound, walking across the antechamber floor to awaken Gwyneth, who rested upright in a fireside chair.

Words were unnecessary because they knew each other's thoughts-they always had. The instant her eyes startled open and gazed into his, he knew she understood that he had failed. She tended to his wound and then, unbelievably, took the baby as her own. Could a blessing called Gwyneth overcome the creature of darkness that he had just discovered behind that bedroom door? He could only hope.

Chapter 5
In Rhian's bedchamber

As told by Rhian
5:00 AM

Rhian climbed exhausted into bed, greatly troubled by what he had just witnessed in Sif's bedroom. How could one explain the glowing red orb without invoking the supernatural? If Rhian's powers of observation were accurate, his wife's crystal instrument had the ability to pleasure, enthrall, protect, cloak, heal and illuminate; and for all Rhian knew, it might also have the capacity to see both past and future! The very thought made him shudder, because if Sif could somehow gain knowledge of his past relationship with Gwyneth by looking into her devil's globe, he and his soul's other half might both be in mortal danger.

His apprehension was quickly overpowered by his weariness. *My sweet Gwyneth, how unexpected and welcome it was to see you again today, after so many years! What I would not give to relive that fine day and that beautiful night two and a half years ago!* A moment later he drifted off into a deep sleep, and in the vivid dream that followed his wish was oddly granted.

***

Rhian recognized the scene immediately; and if the dream held its course without deviating, it

168

would lead him through the events that resulted in his first meeting with the beautiful Gwyneth.

He was riding a horse at a leisurely pace through a meadow on a warm day in autumn, masquerading (as was his custom, on occasion) as a penniless traveler. He loved to venture unaccompanied into the countryside, traveling to all four corners of his beloved Islay, his goal to converse with his people as a peer rather than as their lord. They would often confide in him, usually referencing their thane in a positive light, but sometimes divulging their frustrations and worries about the state of political affairs on the Scottish island. Rhian would always learn much, using the knowledge he gathered to improve his governing skills and enrich the lives of his mostly-loyal subjects.

It was early morning, and although he had spent the night in a lean-to, he felt refreshed and rejuvenated. He steered his horse across the meadow, emerging from the grassy hillock to join a small group of farmers on the main dirt path. Two of them were men who looked to be in their late forties or early fifties, while the other two were lads-both of them in their mid-teens, by appearance. They were in all likelihood two fathers and their sons, probably going to tend to their fields. Each of the two men held hoes and one of the lads carried a shovel, while the other boy, whose muscles attested to his strength, pushed a cart that was packed high with tensely filled burlap bags-*wheat for a late planting, no doubt.*

"Hail, friends," he called out to them from the saddle with a smile. "May I join you as you walk, on this fine September morning?"

"Aye, you may," said one of the men. He was solid and stocky, with a full head of graying hair and a thick beard to match. Rhian dismounted from his horse to walk alongside the four peasants, leading his animal by the reign alongside while he took the hand that had been extended to him in greeting. "I am Donaidh," the farmer said; "and this lad... " (he pointed by way of explanation to the boy with the cart) "... is Fearghas, my son."

"I am very pleased to meet you both."

The other man shook hands with Rhian as well. "I am Tearlach: Donaidh's brother; and this one is *my* son, Ewan."

"I'm Cadman," Rhian fibbed. "I have traveled alone for many days, and I yearn for a bit of company."

"Where are you headed?" asked Donaidh.

"To the coast, to join my brother: a fisherman. Sadly, I lost all of my possessions, except for this old but trusty nag, in a fire, and my brother has kindly offered to take me in."

Donaidh nodded. "These are difficult times, traveler. Our harvest was poor, due to heavy rains in July, and we must plant winter wheat so that we can pay the required tithe to the Thane of Islay."

Rhian felt a pang of remorse. *These good people struggle to survive, yet they bravely strive to meet their obligations.* He took in a breath before continuing. "You are worthy and loyal, good farmer. Perhaps Thane MacDhomhnuill will require less in payments this season, if the harvest was poor."

"Perhaps. He is a noble and just ruler. Regardless, we have our cross to bear, and we would never shirk our duty."

At that moment, there was a sudden commotion on the path ahead of them. They were just reaching the top of a small rise in the hilly terrain, and as such they could not see over to the descending continuation of the path. On the other side, they heard the sound of hoof-beats and the curses of futile pursuers.

Realizing that a skittish horse was most likely heading their way, the small group scrambled to move aside before the animal came galloping over the hill, but without sufficient forewarning, the last minute attempt to avert disaster was only a partial success. Fearghas, finding it difficult to maneuver the heavy and cumbersome grain-laden cart, had hastily abandoned it in his rush to safety such that the wheelbarrow, resting now in the dead center of the path, would represent an unavoidable and dangerous obstacle to the fleeing horse that would momentarily emerge from over the crest of the hill. Meanwhile, Rhian was experiencing his own difficulties. Try as he might, he simply could not persuade his slow-moving mare to evacuate the unhindered dirt roadway for the uninviting tangle of dense brush on the pathway's shoulder.

In a cloud of dusty confusion, the frightened beast came careening over the hill's summit and charged headlong into the farm cart, which clipped the animal's front legs as he attempted, a moment too late, to leap over the obstruction. The airborne

171

horse crashed forcefully into Rhian's nag while she, in turn, fell towards Rhian like a two-ton stone. Knocked backwards, the last thing Rhian remembered was a searing pain at the back of his head as he abruptly fell into black unconsciousness.

When he awoke, still in his dream, some few hours later, Rhian was met by the blurry outline of a face swimming in his field of vision. "Donaidh," Rhian said with some difficulty. His mouth was dry and his head was pounding, so when the farmer offered him a cup of cool water, Rhian accepted it gratefully and drained the contents in a single gulp. He immediately realized that he was lying recumbent on a bed of hay, inside a small and modest barn, with his head and neck resting on a burlap bag stuffed with feathers. With some difficulty, he propped himself partially upright on his elbows with a quiet moan. "What happened to me on the pathway, friend? I remember the galloping horse and his collision with mine, but then nothing."

"Fortunately, traveler, you were thrown backwards to safety by your animal's momentum rather than ending up below her. Both brutes broke their hind legs, and their injuries could not be repaired." His voice trailed off, the implication obvious. "There was nothing we could do for either of them."

Rhian quickly processed this information. "She was a loyal beast, and I shall miss her sorely."

"You cannot complete your journey on foot, friend. I will lend you my mule, *and* my son. I pray you will accept my offer."

172

Rhian was touched by the farmer's kindness. "Aye," he agreed, smiling warmly. "I give you my word that they will both be returned to you safely." Rhian chuckled to himself, knowing full well that he would repay the peasant's kindness with half a dozen horses as well as forgiveness of the next three season's tithes.

"Are you strong enough to join us for supper?"

"Aye, friend." Rhian got up slowly, surprised to feel the room spin as soon as he stood upright, but Donaidh was at his side in an instant, stabilizing him from behind with an arm around his chest. The sensation of dizziness passed quickly.

"I'm fine now," Rhian said quietly. "If you lead, I will follow."

Donaidh released his grip, staying by his side for the first few steps to prevent a fall. Rhian, feeling stronger, walked with sturdy determination towards the barn door.

Donaidh laughed. "You are strong and stubborn, I'll give you that!"

They walked together across a large courtyard of packed dirt to eventually arrive at a modest cottage-house with a thatched roof. Soft wisps of smoke drifted from the chimney into the darkening autumn sky while the promising smell of nourishment swept from the room in a delicious odor, reminding Rhian that he had not eaten for more than twenty-four hours. They entered a single-room living space dominated by a sturdy wooden dining table accented with a bench on each side rather than chairs, its surface loaded with food including a steaming roasted chicken on a large platter, a loaf of bread, a pitcher of ale, and an enormous bowl that was heaped with steaming vegetables. A fireplace with its hearth open on both sides, functioning as a heat source as well as a cooking stove, was situated immediately behind the table in the exact center of the room, with cots lined up behind in cramped, open-style sleeping quarters meant for five.

Donaidh's wife stood on the far side of the table, her ruddy face beaming a smiling welcome, while on either side of her stood Donaidh's son Fearghas, and an attractive girl with blonde hair who was probably seventeen or eighteen years old. Another older girl with rich auburn hair was bent over the fireplace, her back turned as she cooled the smoldering coals with water from a clay jug. Her task completed, the dark haired girl wiped her hands efficiently on her apron and turned, causing Rhian to startle on first sight, his head literally reeling on first sight. *My sweet God in Heaven, she is a beauty!*

"You look peaked, Cadman," the girl's father was saying, his words sounding distant and muted, as if they were being transmitted through the distortion of thick molasses. "Sit you down here, lad." He felt Donaidh's arm on his, easing him down onto the bench on the near side of the table while his wife poured him a mug of ale. Rhian had heard of love as a physical reaction to first visual contact, but never believed it could happen; yet here he was, his mouth dry and his gut wrenching as if he had been kicked by a horse. *This woman is an angel, and as God is my witness I have died and gone to heaven.* "Thank you," he managed to say after composing himself with a sip or two of ale. "I haven't fully recovered yet from my injury, I guess."

"The liquid will surely revive you;" which it did, but slowly, allowing Rhian adequate time to sneak a glance or two at the maiden who had taken her place, standing right next to her fair-haired sister. Her eyes were browner than the richest chocolate, her skin the creamy shade of a pale lily petal, and her teeth as white as a dogwood blossom. She brushed some strands of hair from her forehead seductively-unintended, he felt sure; yet, there seemed to be a connection between them that he knew she shared. Her eyes locked his, dangerously inviting, causing him to disengage his glance and hastily turn his attention back to Donaidh.

"I am better now, thanks to your kind hospitality."

Donaidh clapped him on the back. "Some food should help you too, laddie. Eilidh has cooked our finest chicken to give you strength."

Rhian nodded his thanks to Donaidh's wife. "You are too kind, Lady. I must admit to a strong hunger!"

Donaidh laughed. "Sit down, one and all, and we will sup with our newfound friend." The farmer sat to Rhian's left and Eilidh to his right, while the three children sat on the opposite bench with the stunning brunette, to the thane's delight, sitting directly across from him. "May I introduce my eldest, Gwyneth." Donaidh pointed to the dark-haired beauty, who met Rhian's gaze again to acknowledge the introduction. Did he read excitement in those pools of brown, and passion in those pouty lips? How wonderful it would be to find out. "Caetie is our middle child," Donaidh continued; "and you have already met my son, Fearghas."

"I am truly pleased to meet you all. I am forever in your debt."

"Eat, friend," Donaidh suggested, "and then you will rest again. My home is yours."

Eilidh deftly brandished the cutlery; and when all of the plates had been piled high with chicken, bread and vegetables, Donaidh said a short prayer. Afterwards, they all ate silently, intent on the blessing of nourishment that had been set before them.

Rhian could not help but gaze at the beautiful Gwyneth repeatedly as they ate. As discreetly as possible, he studied her warm bark-colored eyes, her alluring and prominent cheekbones, the sensuous fullness of her lips, and the way the delicate muscles of her neck tapered into the smoothness of both collarbones leading into the ampleness of her bosom below, which was partly exposed due to the cut of her peasant's dress. Her eye caught his for another overwhelming and fleeting second; and he thought-no, he *knew*-that they were meant for each other. He felt desperate to see her alone, but the contact he craved would never happen in such cramped quarters and with the entire family around. He decided to send her a message in the form of a suggestive glance coupled with a carefully chosen comment.

"My thanks, family," he said, as he rose to take his leave and said his parting words. He made eye contact with each of them briefly, but then made sure that his gaze rested on Gwyneth's when he spoke his last. "Perhaps we will have the chance to meet again sometime soon, and share more than a simple evening meal together?" Had she gleaned his meaning? Gwyneth's smile, barely perceptible, told him that she had. Now he would see if she had the boldness to act.

Donaidh led him back to the barn, his lantern illuminating the distance leading to Rhian's makeshift sleeping quarters. He was exhausted, and couldn't help but fall quickly back to sleep despite his hope that he might enjoy a night-time visitor.

***

Rhian was dreaming still, awakening in his imagination with a start to the recollection of how Gwyneth's lips had felt so moist and warm, pressed on his, when she followed through on his subtle invitation on that warm September evening almost two and a half years ago. She was kneeling beside him naked, having already removed her cotton dress before engaging him in a most impassioned kiss.

"Gwyneth... "

"Hush," she answered; and then before he knew it she was straddled on top, lifting his shirt over and off and then reaching below to release his buckle, tossing all of his clothes a few seconds later onto the hay-scattered planks next to her own so that he was as naked as she. With skin touching skin she pressed her body against his with an audacity that he never expected. 'You are mine' her actions said, and he was totally at her command. She eased herself down without speaking a word, her haunches quivering until they learned the rhythm of

177

first intimacy. Her lips trembled on his neck, in control but barely, her breathing as rapid as her heartbeat, her movements synchronized with his until the moment of commingling, which they shared together in a unified whisper. He sat up, his need for her still as urgent as hers for him, pushing her down onto the hay while still engaged but with their positions reversed, with master on top and mistress below until finally they had finished. "Cadman," she sighed dreamily.

"I am not he. Call me Rhian, instead."

He could feel her eyes search his in the incomplete darkness. "Why do you have two names, mysterious stranger?"

"I have much to tell you, but the time is not yet ripe for explanations."

She seemed to accept these words. "Rhian," she said, as if testing how the word sounded when spoken. "It is a fine name, traveler, and one which you share with our kind Thane MacDhomhnuill." She gave him a sidelong glance illuminated by moonlight, an indication that she had quickly guessed his true identity. She was bright as well as beautiful. "I must go," she declared. "My family may awaken, and their questions will be difficult to answer if they find me absent."

He nodded his understanding. "I will dream of you, my love, until the morning light awakens me shortly."

"Sleep well, my darling." She slipped her dress over her head, and without another word she was gone.

***

178

As Fearghas loaded the mule for the two-day journey to Dunyvaig, Rhian and Gwyneth had a moment alone behind a tree under a morning sky that was clear and brisk. "I will send you a message," he said to her quietly between kisses. "It will be delivered along with a gift for your father." She nodded her understanding; and a few moments later, as he and Fearghas led the mule down a gentle embankment to the main road, Rhian looked back and saw that she was crying. He was too. *Very soon, Gwyneth. We will be together very soon!*

***

Rhian continued to sleep, but his dreaming had now become a surrealistic decoupage of distorted images and confused memories. The six steeds he had later gifted to Donaidh galloped in perfect formation, tail to muzzle, each carrying a bag of gold coins representing the three years of tithe forgiveness that he, as thane, had granted Gwyneth's father as thanks for his hospitality on that unforgettable autumn day. Tied to the last horse's tail flapped a letter which promptly disengaged itself, fluttering onto the dusty path where it trembled as though it were alive. The horses disappeared beyond the bend as Rhian bent over to pick up the paper, but it tumbled of its own accord away from him and into a puddle where it sank and completely disappeared.

Rhian rushed over, lowering himself onto hands and knees and peering into the water, where he quickly discovered that he was now watching an image of Gwyneth, who had retrieved the letter and was now reading it, her rich brown eyes moist with tears of joy. In that first of many love letters, Rhian had revealed his identity (although Gwyneth had already correctly guessed that he was the Thane of Islay), professing his undying love for her and asking that she keep their affair secret. He had promised to send Brenhin within a fortnight to bring her secretly to Dunyvaig for their first night-time rendezvous, but he had not been able to wait that long, dispatching his friend and lieutenant just a few days later to retrieve Gwyneth and deliver her safely to his bedroom, in the dead of night. But then, suddenly, as Rhian continued staring into the puddle, he witnessed a change in Gwyneth's expression, and his heart fell. She was holding a *different* letter in her trembling fingers-one that he had penned a full year later and which had started: *my heart is filled with sadness as I write these words.* As she read, Gwyneth's tears became torrential, obscuring her face like a waterfall; and when they finally subsided, Rhian, horrified, found himself staring into *Sif's* eyes in the puddle, rather than into Gwyneth's.

Rhian turned away and tried to run, but his legs were frozen by a demon's spell and the devil herself blocked his pathway, materializing larger than life not 3 paces away from him. Although the air was still, her wild burgundy hair blew across her face, and her flowing black gown flapped noisily against its own heavy fabric until it opened at the front and violently blew off, leaving Sif standing naked, her skin glowing crimson as if consumed by a raging fire underneath its burning surface. She held out her hand, palm up, upon which she held the orb an inch or two at the most away from his face. He saw his own lips reflected in the crystal, and they spoke with his own voice. "Recall ye, mortal, the words you wrote to your soul's other half?"

"Aye."

"Listen, then, as I read them."

"Must I?" He couldn't bear to hear them.

"You must... " and Rhian knew, in his dream, that he had no choice. "My love," he heard himself say, his voice projecting from the depths of the globe itself, "my heart is filled with sadness as I write these words. My duty calls me to wed another, and I cannot keep a mistress. Although our romance must end, you will always be my soul's joy. Your love resides in my heart, and there it will stay until the day I die." The globe, having finished its heart-breaking soliloquy, suddenly burst into flames, pouring upon him the intense heat of guilt that threatened to burn his body into the dust of the ground he stood upon.

How could I betray her? How can I possibly live with myself now? And that's when he awoke with a start in his chambers, no longer dreaming.

***

He knew immediately that he had been awakened by the sound of his bedroom door opening and closing, so he quietly reached for his dagger underneath his pillow. He gripped the hilt of his weapon tightly, removing his covers and swinging his legs over the edge of the bed. In the dead of winter the dawn came late, so it was still pitch black in the room except for a dim semicircle of illumination cast onto the space in front of the massive hearth by the still-burning fire. He peered carefully into the darkness, crouching next to his bed and listening intently for any sound that might indicate the presence of a concealed foe. Rhian had enemies, for certain, and if they had somehow entered his bedroom while he slept, unguarded, they could easily cut his throat as he slumbered. He had ignored Brenhin's repeated advice to post a guard outside his chamber door, but now he thought that perhaps he would reconsider.

He thought he saw a shadow cast vaguely upon the sitting area in front of the fireplace. "Who goes there?" he called out, standing up and raising his dagger in defense. "Show yourself, intruder, and face me in hand-to-hand combat."

The owner of the shadow stepped into the dying light of the fire, and Rhian dropped his dagger in surprise and elation. "Gwyneth!"

"Hush," she whispered, just as she had in the barn so many years before; walking boldly towards him, as gloriously naked now as she was then; pushing him back onto his bed and straddling him before he could protest; and undressing him with the same wordless determination that she had employed before, on that warm September night when they had initially met. As she lowered herself down, her body shuddering with the initial contact, she whispered in his ear. "This is our destiny, told to me by a soothsayer. Give yourself to me, lover."

And he did.

Chapter 6
In Sif's bedchamber

As told by Sif
6:00 AM

Sif stood naked in front of a roaring fire that her maidservant had just stoked, the white flames impacting little on the iciness of her heartless soul. *Enough heat*, she thought while moving away from the flames and over to the colder atmosphere on the other side of the room, where her orb lay dormant on a red satin cushion on her dresser. She much preferred the lower temperature, even more now since she had been forced to leave her frozen Scandinavian home for this intolerably temperate climate and a pitiful thane that she had been urged to take as husband, at least in name.

She had never desired a mate, after all, but had agreed to the arranged marriage only because her union with the Gaul had been condoned by her Coven. Her Wiccan compatriots were anxious to extend their base of power beyond the confines of their icy island by installing Sif and an as yet unconceived demon-prince in Scotia; and for this reason, they had urged her to accept Olaf's political proposition. Prior to her departure, though, she needed to create her 'orb' in a final rite of passage marking her advancement from novice to sorceress.

Although it took the appearance of crystal, the globe was actually transmuted energy with no 'physical' substance. It was the focal point of her occult strength that she would use, when necessary, to amplify her powers and facilitate the practice of her dark arts. Sif's orb was multi-talented. It could see into the past and predict the future; it could protect and heal; it could excite and stimulate; it could injure and kill; and, most importantly, it could focus and consolidate. As an extension of herself, it was really her 'better half': a true husband, if truth be told, in more ways than strictly spiritual.

Her training as a sorceress began when she was barely sixteen, after her observant handmaiden, Enid, had noticed a talent in the young girl. Enid was perhaps ten years older than the young princess; and with time, as the servant tended to her mistress' every need, they became close friends. Sif rapidly matured into a fiery-haired sensuous beauty with a soul that burned with sinister heat. Enid correctly sensed the girl's supernatural energy and offered to introduce her to the Wiccan masters to begin her tutoring in the black arts.

"Young mistress," Enid said, "your gifts are hidden to most, but obvious and transparent to my discerning eye."

Sif cocked her head. "I understand you not, Enid."

"There is awesome power in your touch and in your eyes. A powerful enchantress lies dormant within you, and calls to be awakened!"

Sif remembered the heat of excitement that had rushed through her veins when she heard Enid's words. "What must I do to become what you see in me?"

"You must do what I did." And so Sif's 'sponsor' led her that very same night through the darkness of the secret tunnels under the castle, the handmaiden's own blazing energy orb lighting their way. Each night, for the next two years, Enid escorted Sif through the confusing maze of passageways under the frozen mountainside for her tutorials within a central cavern with the 'Great Ones.' The three Masters gave freely of their diabolical knowledge; and soon, Sif learned that the supernatural and the physical were inextricably linked, until finally she reached the point of readiness for her demonic initiation.

"It is time for your final task," Enid told her one night in February, just a few weeks before the emissaries from Islay were scheduled to arrive to make the marriage contract final. "The Masters have determined that you are prepared; and tonight, dear sister, you will make your own crystal power globe. You will take the orb with you to Scotia, and use it to enslave your betrothed and his entire kingdom."

Sif took a breath in. She had worked hard, and her efforts would finally bear the fruit of her labors. "I am ready," she proclaimed. "Tell me what I must do!"

"You will let the three great Masters help you construct your orb. They will draw out your energy to make a most powerful crystal while you lie naked on the ritual slab, with the entire Coven surrounding you to bear witness."

Sif nodded. "Take me now, Enid, to my final test!"

Her friend led Sif down the winding passageway and into the familiar Coven's den for her initiation and the long-awaited creation of her very own energy globe. Sif was disrobed in front of the gathered audience by the three great Warlocks, who then proceeded to lead her solemnly to a knee-high granite altar where they signaled her to lie on her back, in full lengthwise-view of the Coven. Her facilitators were dressed in flowing robes and wore masks depicting the faces of the three most potent of the masculine Nordic gods.

"We, the Deities of old, present this initiate, who has successfully completed her training," the Master disguised as Odin announced. "Watch our sister goddess of the Underworld merge her black energy with that of Odin's to create an all-powerful energy crystal."

There was a murmur of approval from the two-dozen onlookers as each warlock took their positions around the table. 'Thor', the god of War, stood at Sif's head and grasped her upper arms while 'Freyr', the horned God of fertility, stationed himself at her feet, where he gripped her ankles with his bulging muscles, the both of them securing her limbs in four-point restraint in preparation for the ordeal that would shortly follow. 'Odin', the ruler of Valhalla, knelt facing the Coven directly astride Sif's navel and the bareness of her most intimate spot, touching the back of both of his hands lightly onto the flatness of her tensing stomach and pelvis, palms facing up. In a few short moments, Sif knew, he would initiate a physical and psychic connection with Sif's most primal core to release, harness and capture Sif's awesome supernatural energy and power.

"In Hecate's name," Sif gasped, surprised by the force of the spasms that had suddenly gripped her midsection, causing beads of sweat to boil on her quivering skin. Her muscles contracted under pinned-down limbs and feverish flesh as a swirling mass of crimson vapor emanated from her loins, rapidly concentrating into a misty sphere in the cup of 'Odin's' outstretched palms. "I command thee to solidify," she ordered, saying the words with guttural emphasis at the exact and proper time, just as her Masters had previously instructed. In response, the gaseous cloud quickly hardened into a shell of ice. "Now," she whispered, calmer now since the excruciating pain that had wracked her body just a few seconds before had magically dissipated; and accordingly, with a deafening roar and a blinding flash of light, the orb's icy exterior was instantly replaced with a glimmering sphere of solid crystal that 'Odin' placed delicately on Sif's navel.

"Release her," he ordered; and the other two did, giving Sif the freedom to reach down and touch her newly-formed lover. The orb's surface was soft, not hard, and begged her for contact, whispering seductively in her head with such conviction that she had no choice but to comply, right there under the scrutiny of her peers.

Her globe of power had been forged from the lewdness of her naked body not yet a year gone by; and now, as Sif stood in front of her dresser mirror, she couldn't help but admire that same nudity in the clear reflecting glass. Her pregnancy and the subsequent trauma of delivering twins had left no sign on her enticing flesh, thanks to the healing power of her magical sphere. Her stomach was no longer protuberant; her labia were no longer

187

swollen; and the painful rip on the outside of her vagina had been miraculously healed-all this, from one simple touch of her incomparable crystal on injured flesh and skin! She caressed her breasts, already engorged with milk that she would never use for the useless girl-child, moving her hands slowly downward over her tight stomach and further, rotating around and looking over her shoulder at the perfection of her waist, hips and thighs as seen from the back. How delicious she looked; and no one could have her except the orb, with one exception allowed only once three seasons past, with the sole purpose of planting a seed in her fertile womb and building a demonic empire right here on earth.

She scoffed, thinking of her newborn daughter with contempt. "What a useless waste of time and labor," she had said to her crystal just an hour or so ago, while she was mentally entranced and physically engaged behind closed doors, where no one dared to breech her privacy.

Yes, my sweet, the orb had cooed while she was 'under'. *The child will be just like her father, and those attributes will never serve our dark purpose. Hers is a bland and strikingly human core. The boy, you should know, would have been a great warlock-perhaps even the great Unifier. But fear not, there will be another son.*

"Must I?" she had asked, cringing at the thought of bedding the thane again so that he could father the 'great one'.

You must. I will allow you another commingling and ensure its success.

So she would. It would be worth the five minutes with him on top; and one thing for sure-he would be an easy mark. She had severed their sexual relations more than nine months ago now, after a single coupling, so he would be primed and ready for another chance to sample her secrets. Who wouldn't lust for her attentions, especially after so many months of frustrating abstinence? She moved her hands, again, over her youthful curves, reaching for her orb and removing him from his pillow, saying 'wake up' with a tender kiss on his sleeping shell, which was actually seductively soft even though it looked thoroughly hard. "It's time to consult you again, my crystal counselor," she announced out loud, gazing deeply into the awakened depths of the globe's concentrated energy and feeling him draw her in like a vortex. Sometimes he would simply talk to her, but more urgent matters required scene depiction like this; and when she was completely 'in', she realized that the globe had taken her back in time, to the day of her arrival at Dunyvaig Castle last July.

After their quiet wedding ceremony in the stone-cold castle in Isafjordhur, Rhian returned immediately home, leaving his new bride to gather her new household over the next two leisurely months of spring-become-summer before she finally decided it was time to join him in Islay. Becoming pregnant on their wedding night, Sif's unborn son demanded an introduction to his kingdom; so she traveled with a handful of domestics across the North Atlantic, arriving in mid-July at a shoreline harbor where a dozen of Rhian's soldiers had been dispatched to greet her. Three hours later the party finally neared Dunyvaig Castle on the far side of the island, perched on a cliff overlooking Lagavulin Bay, the sun setting as they approached and the shadow of the looming fortress reaching out to them like fingers. The castle's highest tower spiraled high into the sky: an inky silhouette against the backdrop of an orange, setting sun that seemed to literally touch on the clouds above. *The threat of retribution lurks in this tower, methinks.* Sif clutched her globe tightly under her cloak, feeling reassured by the tingling power she could feel emanating from the contact on her palm. *My crystal lover knows. This place cannot conceal its pain from his all-seeing eye.*

She turned brusquely to the lieutenant that rode by her side. "Warrior, have you a name?"

"Brenhin, my Lady," the man replied tersely.

"Brenhin," she began, gazing distractedly at the tower that emerged like a powerful weapon from the castle's armored body. "This spiraling tower intrigues me. Is it used for a lookout, or for some other secret purpose?"

"The highest battlements provide a sweeping view, Lady Sif. From that vantage point, we can easily spot an enemy's approach, by land or by sea, from a ten mile distance surrounding us."

"Quite unnecessary, I should think. Olaf provides his protection, does he not?"

"Yes, my Lady, but Norway's alliance was only recently formed. These battlements you gaze upon were constructed many years ago. When our thane commissioned the builders, he ordered this towering lookout so that his vision would reach up to the heavens, for all to see."

190

She nodded. "This tower has piqued my interest. Is there a room at the top that I could inhabit?"

"There *is* a room, but it is our thane's private sanctuary. It is small, and sparsely decorated-hardly a lady's bedroom."

"Ah, what a shame. Methinks I would have been quite comfortable in the vulture's lofty nest."

"My lord has prepared a luxurious suite of rooms for you in the east wing. You will be very satisfied with your new quarters, my Lady."

They rode the remaining distance in silence. *This tower will play some role in my evil task here-of this I feel quite sure.*

Night had fallen as they reached the castle. The gates had been opened, the drawbridge was down, and their way had been prepared; but as she watched herself ride into the outer courtyard, the orb abruptly switched to a different scene in his portrayal of her past. Now she saw herself seated at a centrally appointed table at the front of the castle's banquet hall with Rhian at her one side and Brenhin on the other. A single column of tables ran perpendicular to the royal grouping and overflowed with victuals and refreshments. The room buzzed with activity, as countless servants attended to the demands and needs of over three hundred guests who were attending the welcome reception.

"The people of Islay have been anxiously awaiting your arrival," Brenhin was saying. "They love their thane dearly, and wish nothing more for him than his happiness... and yours."

This Brenhin is subtle in his insolence. I have no concern for the peasants in this foreign land, nor

191

do I care about the happiness of my pitiful husband–and he knows it. Her crystal globe had assured her that her betrothal to the thane was simply a means to an end. Her union with Rhian, consummated two months ago with one hasty but successful 'insemination', had already produced a son with the potential to become the great Wiccan Unifier foretold in legends, whose fluttering movements she felt nightly in her newly-pregnant womb. Brenhin awaited her response, but she would wield the unspoken weapon of silence for a moment longer. Sif raised her glass slowly, sipping her wine with measured leisure. When she finally opened her mouth to speak, she stifled a yawn. "And why, pray tell, do these lowly people love him so?"

"Rhian is kind and fair minded, but also a fearsome warrior and a powerful leader. Why should they not love him?"

Deciding that his rhetorical question did not deserve an answer, Sif drank quietly from her cup as Rhian acknowledged the compliment. "Thank you, Brenhin. You are my loyal friend, and my most deserved lieutenant."

Sif gazed at Rhian, inspecting the man that she viewed as an obligation. *He is certainly handsome, but his kind and forgiving spirit detracts greatly from his appeal.* She studied his blonde hair, his strong full lips, his clean-shaven cheek, and his sky-blue eyes. *He has done his job, and I will suffer his company now only outside the bedroom; but when my son is born, he will no longer be useful. I will strangle him with a most potent curse as soon as my child lives and breathes, and this pitiful thane will die in his sleep with no one being the wiser.*

192

She looked casually around the banquet hall, studying the guests who were busy eating at the tables as well as the servants who attended them-and that's when one of the peasant servers caught her eye. The girl's skin looked too ruddy, as if it had been darkened intentionally with an extract or a dye; her hair looked too light, somehow; and as she bent over to retrieve a platter of meat from a portly nobleman, Sif caught a glimpse of some padding underneath the girl's skirt. Why was she disguised? It mattered not, yet curiosity caused Sif's gaze to linger until the girl finally looked towards the head table with eyes that were a rich brown in color, giving the enchantress a perfect opportunity to practice the 'strangle spell' that she would eventually use on her witless husband. *What fun. These insignificant insects must learn to fear me, and I will start with this meaningless peasant girl.*

The servant, unable to look away, shuddered, her eyes wide with fear as the stranglehold gripped her heart, choking the life out of her bit by bit, the intensity building towards the final asphyxiation-but no, it wasn't worth it. Sif would save the lethal endgame for someone who actually mattered; so she looked away, releasing her silent hold on the girl's soul and allowing her to live another day. The would-be victim was visibly shaken and nervously gathered her platter, scurrying away to the safety of the kitchen and beyond, pleasing Sif's thirst for intimidation, at least. "Why are you showing me this?" she asked her crystal lover.

Because the girl will play a disastrous role in your drama, but only if you do not stop her. Watch, mistress. The globe showed the servant girl again,

193

but this time depicted her some moments *before* Sif had reached out with her death-grip. The peasant was making eye contact with someone *else* at the head of the table, her face beaming with the hot flush of desire, yearning and love. "Does she lust for the lieutenant called Brenhin, orb?"

No, she desires your husband. They were lovers, and are still.

The scene changed, abruptly. Sif, no longer reliving her arrival banquet, was transported by her supernatural appendage into the here and now, where she stood invisibly in the thane's quarters. Rhian and a dark-haired, fair skinned beauty lay naked together, ardent and impassioned, in his *bed* of all places! It only took Sif a moment to make the connection; and in a flash, she knew. "He lies with the maiden from the banquet, no longer in disguise-does he not?"

He does, at this very moment. Beware, enchantress. You must kill her, before she saves him and destroys you.

The anger seethed in Sif's spleen. "Who is she?"

Her name is Gwyneth.

"This Gwyneth shall pay with her life." Sif shook herself out of the trance, placing the orb back on his pillow on her dresser, where he became instantly dormant. "In fact, all *three* of them will pay," the witch announced, deciding hastily that it would not only be Gwyneth who would suffer the dire consequences of her ill-intentioned betrayal, but Rhian and his powerless child as well. Sif would find another warrior to inseminate her-the cocky lieutenant Brenhin, perhaps? No one was irreplaceable.

But then she thought again. This Gwyneth she would certainly kill, and the baby too-but Rhian would live, because a more perfect punishment she could not imagine. *Oh, the heartache he will feel when he discovers his daughter and his lover, both dead, with only himself to blame.* What a beautiful and flawlessly cruel idea.

"He will live, most certainly-a long and tortured life," she commented out loud to her reflection in the mirror. *Yes, he will live. As Hecate is my evil mistress, the thane shall live.*

Chapter 7
In Rhian's bedchamber

As told by Gwyneth
7:00 AM

Gwyneth had fallen asleep in Rhian's arms immediately after their lovemaking, but now she awoke as the first light of day began to lighten the sky outside the chamber window. Her lover still slept, so she gently disengaged herself from his embrace, careful not to disturb him as she climbed out of his bed, walking over to lay some logs on the fire and sitting down in front of it as the dry wood quickly took flame. The heat felt good on her naked skin, and she closed her eyes contentedly.

She could hardly believe she was here with him now. Her place, she knew, was at his side; but until today, she had given up all hope that they could possibly be reunited. But what would happen to them now? He loved her, she knew; but since his marriage to Sif had been arranged politically, Rhian would never be able to cast off the Viking princess and take Gwyneth as his lady instead without threatening the peace and safety of the entire kingdom. Even if the union could somehow be annulled (which Gwyneth recognized as impossible), the vindictive woman whose gaze had frozen Gwyneth's deepest soul in the banquet hall would never let bygones be bygones. All of the rumors about Sif were true, which meant that if Rhian rejected his wife for another, the repercussions would definitely take a supernatural form.

She thought back on their romantic history, and the last time they had seen each other, over two years ago now. She sighed. Neither of them had known, of course, that this rendezvous (which had occurred immediately prior to Rhian's meeting with Olaf, the King of Mann and the Isles) was destined to be their last, on that early autumn day when the nights were cool but the days were still warm. Their romance, by necessity, was a decidedly quiet affair, their trysts always cloaked in secrecy, usually facilitated by Rhian's trusted friend and lieutenant, Brenhin, who would whisk her away in the dead of night and deposit her happily into her lover's royal bed. On other occasions Rhian would appear unannounced and without warning, his appearance disguised somehow so that he would not be recognized as the island kingdom's thane; and then they would retreat together, discreetly, to some private location or a distant inn or tavern, where they would sometimes slyly play the role of peasant husband and wife to the unsuspecting innkeeper. Although these adventures were always rich and exciting, she longed for the day when their relationship could be open and transparent. She even thought that perhaps he might eventually take her as his true and legal wife rather than keeping her as his mistress.

On that early morning in October, Gwyneth had risen from her cot in the corner of her family's tiny cottage well before sunrise, since it was her turn to milk the cows. Careful not to wake the still-sleeping household, she pulled off her nightshirt and slipped on a simple cotton smock, feeling the fabric touch her naked skin when she moved, just like Rhian's imagined fingers. She made her way quietly across the room, lighting an oil lamp and holding it in front of her as she stepped outside, traversing the dark and deserted courtyard with lantern-light as her guide and reaching her destination quickly, only to discover with shock that the barn door was more than halfway open.

She stopped dead in her tracks. Perhaps she hadn't latched it? That type of careless mistake could easily lead to the escape of their livestock, which she prayed had not occurred yet; so, with due haste and dropping the lamp on the ground so it would not impede her, she rushed inside, realizing as she did so that she would need the light she left outside to inspect the dark interior. She was in the process of turning on her heel to retrieve her light-source when someone grabbed her from behind, clamping a large and forceful palm over her mouth to stifle her scream of alarm.

He pushed her against the wall purposefully, lifting her smock above the waist with his free hand to expose her from the backside, his body tensing against her in response to the feel of her nudity underneath. "Quiet now," he whispered, sliding his hand off her lips and placing it on her waist just opposite his other, using his strength to secure her while he took her right then and there, surrounded in darkness with no one around except the cows and the chickens to bear witness to her unexpected subjugation. When the conquest reached its inexorable conclusion, he spun her around so that she could face her well-known assailant.

"Rhian," she said, embracing him with her arms around his neck and standing on tiptoes with her lips pressed against his in a welcome-kiss that seemed to last forever.

"My love," he eventually replied, holding her close. "Did I surprise you?"

"Yes. What are you doing here, darling? You *never* visit me like this, undisguised."

"I have been summoned to meet with the King of the Isles," he said quietly. "Since your farmhouse is on the way, I thought I'd make a quick stop."

"Why are you meeting with the King?" The logical explanation came to mind. "Is he calling you to war?"

"I have heard of no such plans, although Olaf Godredsson is unpredictable, self-serving, and ambitious. With Morsel, anything's possible."

She shuddered with dread. "If you go away to fight on some distant battlefield, I will simply die!"

He touched her face with gentle hands. "Worry not, sweet one. I will return to you always, even if I should perish."

"If that should happen, I would take my own life in order to join you in eternity."

They enjoyed each other once more, on the same bed of hay where she had originally seduced him; and when he rode away shortly thereafter with the rising sun at his back, horse and rider disappearing over the hill at the edge of the farmstead with her waving happily goodbye, she fully expected that she would see him again soon... which of course she didn't. Instead, it was barely a week later when she received a letter that shattered her world and decimated all hope that her life from here on out would be at all worth living. Sitting now in front of the fire in Rhian's bedchamber, she could hardly believe that they had been reunited after so many long years of separation, the joy followed by heartache of that final meeting clinging to her memory like the long lost remnant of sleep. All at once she felt unbearably weary, so getting up she made her way back to Rhian's bed, crawling under the covers beside him and falling asleep immediately with the grateful warmth of his body close against her.

The dream began with the sound of waves crashing behind her. She was standing on a rock-strewn beach facing a steep sheer cliff with his castle behind her, the granite fortress essentially one and the same with the near-black boulders and rocks from which it emerged, its silhouette blending as well with the slate-colored cloud-cover above and the swirling sea of murky grey below. In typical dream-like fashion, the castle belonged to Rhian, and yet it didn't. Gwyneth strained her neck, looking upward at the battlements and noticing that they were strangely deserted. *How desolate and lonely. There has been some tragedy here*, she realized, *and now the castle has been abandoned.* At this same moment she became troubled by the placement of the castle high above, on the summit of a dizzying rocky precipice. *What a far, far drop it would be from the top of that highest castle tower to the rocks and water below.*

Is that what had happened? With horror she understood that someone *had* fallen-but whom? Looking frantically around on the rocky beach where she stood, she didn't see a body; and that's when the voice behind her spoke.

"It has been moved."

She spun around, finding that she was being addressed by a soldier dressed head-to-toe in the accoutrements of warfare, his armor painted in various shades of glaring, screaming red. His helmet and visor, which completely concealed his face, throbbed like a heartbeat synchronized to his words. "What has been moved?" She moved closer and noticed that she could not look directly at him without squinting. Although the sky was dark and dreary, the brilliant metallic crimson covering his body gleamed like it was made of shards of glass reflecting the glaringly absent sun.

"The body has, my lady. It has been taken to its final resting place."

She approached closer, so that now she could actually reach out and accost him. "Who has fallen from the tower?" she screamed, pounding on the blood-red steel of his chest plate with both fists. "Tell me now, soldier! Who has fallen?"

"Enter and you shall see." The metal instantly melted into blood, which flash-coagulated into a door stained the shockingly-bright color of hemorrhage. It somehow knew that she was loath to touch it, so it opened itself with a creak and a groan, allowing her to cross the threshold with a single step whereupon she found that she had suddenly been stripped naked and was walking alone down a cold, alabaster marble hallway. From a distance, she saw that Rhian, naked as well, stood waiting for her at the end of the corridor, standing in front of the entrance to a spiraling stone staircase. When she

201

reached him he took her hand, and she knew instantly where he planned on leading; so she followed, calmly, up and up and up, until finally, one hundred and ninety nine steps later, they had reached a small room, scantly furnished but warmed by a small fire that burned in a corner hearth.

"This room and my soul are one and the same, and they are both yours; but in the commingling you have been placed in grave danger." Rhian's face was etched with worry.

"Who fell from the tower?" She knew at the same moment of asking that it had been her.

"I cannot say, but you may see." Suddenly she was standing outside on the tower's balcony dangerously close to the waist-high stone railing, a strong wind singing through the cracks and battlements and touching on her naked skin with icy belligerence. She peered over cautiously, noticing a letter written in Rhian's penmanship fluttering in an icy up-draft. Curious to read what he had written, she reached out to grab it, losing her balance in the doing, while at the same moment the piece of parchment transformed into a gigantic osprey that dived downward at a speed at least ten times faster than her slow-motion fall, using its six-foot wings to ensure that the journey down would end more happily for the bird than it would for her. Toppling over the edge, Gwyneth's shoulder and hip struck a narrow three-foot wide drainage ledge located five or six feet below the edge of the tower's rim, the momentum causing her to bounce outward, her body twisting and rolling in the empty nothingness for an excruciating second until gravity started to pull her forcefully downward. "Rhian," she screamed over and over in her nightmare, feeling oddly detached, much more like an observer rather than the victim, tumbling wildly through the bitterly frigid air while the landscape approached her in a jumbled chaotic blur, her nudity covered with goosebumps and her limbs stiffer than blocks of ice. He answered her with a voice that sounded both far away and close at hand-because of course he was calling her awake rather than answering her in the dream.

"Gwyneth!" She awoke with a start on Rhian's bed, shivering with both fear and cold because the warm feather comforter had been pulled hastily off her naked and vulnerable body. Rhian was standing next to the bed, dressing hurriedly. "Gwyneth, you must hide!" Someone was pounding on the door. "If they discover you like this, naked in my bed, we will both pay a deadly price."

She pushed herself up and off the mattress, running to the corner of the room where she squeezed behind a large mahogany armoire which would easily serve the purpose of concealment. Rhian, in the meantime, had walked cautiously to the door, opening it a crack to converse quietly with the caller on the other side.

"What is it, Bridget?" she heard him ask.

"It's Aibhilin!" the midwife cried. "She's gone, my Lord!"

"Gone? How could that be?"

"She was in her cradle when we last checked. Somebody must have taken her!"

Suddenly, Gwyneth knew. *The tower! Sif has taken Aibhilin to the tower!* She rushed from her hiding place, unconcerned now with appearances or her state of undress. "The baby has been taken to the tower, Rhian, with ghastly and evil purpose!" She rushed passed him, throwing the door open and pushing Bridget aside, yelling: "I must save her!" over her shoulder as she hurried down the main corridor, realizing that her naked body was still covered in goosebumps even though her blood pumped hot with feverish purpose. She heard Rhian's footsteps following closely behind her, and prayed to God as they ran that it was not too late.

Chapter 8
On the castle tower

As told by Rhian, Sif and Gwyneth
8:00 AM

Rhian overtook Gwyneth at the base of the tower stairs, stopping her with a hand on her shoulder and spinning her around before she could begin a frantic ascent up the winding and seemingly endless staircase. "Gwyneth, explain!"

"We have very little time!" she panted, looking anxiously up the stairwell, and attempting without success to free herself from the strong grip of his hands on her shoulders. "For God's sake, release me Rhian!" She looked pleadingly into his eyes. "We might already be too late to save her!"

"I don't understand."

"Sif has taken Aibhilin to the top! We must stop her, Rhian, because there is murder in her heart!"

"She wouldn't dare!"

"I have seen the evil in her eyes, and visions of what will come to pass if we do not intervene. We must hurry, Rhian, before Aibhilin falls to her death at the witch's hands!"

The word jolted him, because he knew it was true. *Sif is a witch.* Releasing Gwyneth abruptly, he dashed passed her onto the stairs behind, taking three steps at a time so that he might reach the tower's summit before the unspeakable happened. Gwyneth was following, close behind at first, but he quickly outpaced her. Soon, he could barely hear her echoing footsteps far behind.

His legs ached. How many stairs had he climbed already, and how many did he still have left to go? He rushed onward, a hundred steps behind him and just under a hundred yet ahead. He started to sweat, despite the cold; and blinking to clear his vision, he noticed the final landing now through eyes that were blurred by the moisture of his own perspiration, the first rays of the winter morning sun coming from underneath and around the door leading into his tower room. He leapt, fearless, onto the solid stone platform, and without hesitation pushed open the door, rushing in without thinking, primed and prepared to act immediately on his daughter's behalf, regardless of the danger and any resulting consequence. The sunrise was a burning yellow ball, hovering on the horizon to cast its brilliant glare over the balcony railing and through the open window, directly into his eyes. Temporarily blinded, he couldn't react quickly enough to neutralize the ambush.

Sif stood across the room, directly in front of the open doorway that led to the balcony, the sunlight behind her forming a sinister halo around the dark outline of her silhouette. He heard the door behind him respond to its angled engineering, closing itself firmly behind him and preventing retreat, should that recourse become necessary. He could not see Sif's face, but he had no difficulty recognizing the gleaming object that she held in front of her, in her outstretched palms. Her orb looked like a miniature sun, glowing inferno-red in the cradle made by its mistress' hands, streams of combustion jumping from it like solar sunspots: the harbinger, it seemed, of some kind of hell-born conflagration that threatened to erupt in flames at any moment. The object looked so hot that Rhian found himself wondering how Sif could hold it without suffering third degree burns.

"I have been expecting you, my foolhardy husband," she said triumphantly.

"Where is Aibhilin?" Rhian took three steps forward as he spoke, but stopped dead in his tracks when Sif extended the object towards him like a weapon. In response to Sif's murmured order, the orb burned noticeably brighter, its smoky rays shining directly upon him, encircling him with cursed crimson tendrils that immediately bound him with a devil's spell. He felt as if a two-ton weight had been dropped on his shoulders, and he fell to his knees. *I can't move!* He willed his aching and burning limbs to respond by standing back up, but they answered now to another master.

"You are helpless," Sif sneered. "The power of my orb is limitless, and your body is now mine to command, due to my crystal's magic."

"What have you done with Aibhilin? Where is my child?"

"You are too late to save her, I fear. The poor, helpless infant is balanced on the brink of the precipice, and in a moment, she will roll off. What a shame. I'm afraid that no one but you will grieve when she passes from this world into the next." Her chilling words rang in his ears with the finality of a death sentence as he struggled to breathe, his vision fading quickly into the blank emptiness of eternity. *She is killing me and I am truly helpless. God save me*. Prone now rather than kneeling, the room turned grey during his last moments of consciousness while he heard Sif's voice in his head, replying to his final thoughts. "Oh, you will not die, I assure you. I want you alive."

***

Sif gazed with satisfaction at her defeated prey, whose respirations were barely visible and whose lips were painted with a pallor that mimicked death itself as he rested motionless on the cold stone floor, paralyzed and powerless. What an effortless victory she had just won against the pitiful excuse for a warlord, but she had expected no less from her globe of power, whose supernatural grip remained in place around her victim's muscular neck. "Make sure he lives," she told the orb; and in response, the churning cloud of vile energy in her hands instantly changed colors, pulsing now in dark blue subservience rather than the previous, commanding scarlet.

Now Rhian cannot interfere with my plans for the baby, and the mistress. She looked over her shoulder, her eyes squinting to see beyond the glare of the rising sun to confirm that the child was still balanced tenuously on the stone balcony railing, lying on her back just as Sif had left her only a few moments earlier. Aibhilin's tiny limbs flayed helplessly in the air, instinctively countering the invisible assault of the blustery January wind with limited success; perilously swaying back and forth on the brink of the ledge, her weak and high-pitched cries barely audible over the howl of the frigid wintery blast. The thane's helpless daughter still lived, but not for long. If she didn't fall to her death soon, her fragile body (which was loosely wrapped in a thin infant's mantle) would surely succumb to exposure. *Either way, she will not die directly by my own hand,* Sif's twisted mind rationalized. Not that she was averse to murder, but executing her own flesh and blood reflected a blackness that even Sif was unwilling to face. *This method leaves me innocent of the actual deed.* She studied her hands, and the orb whispered the same conclusion in her head. *There is no blood on them, my darling. Your hands are clean.*

Sif walked back through the balcony door, preparing herself for phase two of her vengeful plan, which involved entrapping the thane's lover. If she executed this next step successfully, Rhian would witness both of them falling to their deaths from the tower, the trauma of the double murder scarring him for life, breaking his will forever and making him as malleable as a lump of clay in Sif's manipulative hands. Where was she, though? Sif had envisioned Gwyneth following loyally behind her man, running down the long hallway and up the tower stairs to offer her tremulous assistance; but if so, she should have arrived by now. Had she remained behind, cowering in fright under her lover's bedsheets? That seemed more likely, in retrospect-an action that closely fit the girl's mousy and incurably timid character. She glanced down at her simmering blue orb. *Summon the harlot now, globe; and when she arrives you will release the thane from his unnatural sleep, just in time to see his one-and-only begging for mercy as I use your energy to throw her off this highest turret to her well-deserved death!*

The orb, again becoming a shockingly sanguine red, pulsed happily while Sif closed her eyes, integrating her psyche seamlessly with that of her paranormal appendage. *Come to the tower, maiden.* Sif's voice and energy globe became one and the same, chanting in harmony with words that only Gwyneth could hear. *Make haste and come now, maiden, because your lover is dying and only you can save him!*

Little did Sif know that at that very moment, Gwyneth was waiting on the other side of the landing doorway, preparing for action.

***

Gwyneth stood with her back and one ear pressed against the wood and both hands tensely gripping the door latch, catching her breath for a moment after her frantic sprint to the top of the stairs. Rhian, who was much more accustomed to physical exertion, had easily won the race, arriving a full three or four minutes before her. *I must help him*, she thought, but caution warned her to wait a moment and assess the situation; so here she stood, listening intently to a flurry of commotion on the other side of the tower door *and* to a strange voice that had just started talking in her head, saying: *make haste, maiden; your lover is dying!*

Gwyneth responded immediately, taking in a deep breath and drawing upon every ounce of her emotional and physical strength to throw herself forcefully against the wooden door, unlatching it suddenly so that she literally exploded into the room, screaming at the top of her lungs and barreling directly into Sif, who was taken completely off guard because of her complete immersion in an apparent telepathic trance. They tumbled together onto the cold stone floor, rolling like one chaotic entity through the balcony doorway and onto the mile-high terrace. Gwyneth, whose intuition told her that much of Sif's power was derived from the burning crystal that she was holding in her hands, prayed that the impact of her tackle had disengaged the globe from its owner-which, thankfully, it had. With elation, Gwyneth looked back into the tower room and saw that the orphaned sphere of energy had rolled with quiet discontent near Rhian's motionless body, the tragic significance of her lover's immobility taking a split second to hit home. "What have you done to him!" she screamed, her voice hardly audible over the forlorn and lamenting cry of the frigid January wind.

"Enough, and more," the witch cackled. Enraged, Gwyneth gripped both hands around Sif's throat and squeezed as hard as she could; but before she could finish, she noticed movement on the railing, off to the left, and released her choke-hold immediately. *It's Aibhilin and she's still alive! What kind of a monster would place a child in such jeopardy, let alone her own flesh and blood?* Gwyneth knew what she had to do; so without hesitation, she rushed to prevent a disaster that was already on its way to a dreadful conclusion-because well before she could arrive at the turret railing as the baby's savior, she watched Rhian's daughter

211

disappear, rolling off the edge to fall into the gusting wind and to her death.

"No," Gwyneth cried, unable to ignore the call of her maternal instinct, which illogically ordered her to leap over the railing to retrieve the lost infant. Without even breaking her stride or considering the lethal consequences, she levered her body with outstretched arms and cleared the edge easily, but with horror found herself at gravity's mercy on the other side of her suicide-jumper's arc. *I am falling to my death*, she thought; *and no one in this world or the next will be able to save me.*

***

Rhian awoke in a confused daze, lying face down on the cold stone floor. His cheek was pressed to the hard grey granite, and his head swam with the dizzying remnant of near asphyxiation. The restraints of Sif's binding spell had clearly been loosened, since his limbs, although numb, now moved easily. He slowly and cautiously pushed himself off the floor and onto his hands and knees, satisfied that he would soon be able to support his full weight on his quickly recovering legs.

As he shook off the fog, his eyes focused first on the three or four feet in his immediate field of vision, where his gaze rested immediately and with surprise onto Sif's deadly energy globe, which pulsed with soft blue seduction not even six inches from his right hand. He obviously wouldn't be able to channel the crystal's powerful energy, but having it in his possession would definitely give him the upper hand so he reached out and grabbed it, rising quickly to his feet at the exact same moment. The soothing blue appearance of the witch's tool was a cruel and misleading deception because it sizzled in his grip like a smoking ball of dry ice; but despite the excruciating pain, which cut like a saber from his hand to his shoulder, he clutched the orb with determination, staggering forward and finally reaching the balcony without a small amount of effort. His entire arm throbbed as the evil humors from the swirling orb penetrated into his pores like a poison. *I won't last long at this rate.*

Rhian scanned the deserted stone railings with a sinking heart, dropping to his knees in defeat. "My sweet Aibhilin," he sobbed, noticing Sif for the first time as she rose from her prone position on the platform to stand facing her husband defiantly, but with her eyes fixed with concern on the globe that he still clutched in one hand.

"You have lost, husband," she stated in a very uncertain tone of voice.

Rhian recognized his advantage, holding the globe high into the air so Sif could not misinterpret the leverage; mustering every ounce of his strength to stand tall, with his body silently screaming in painful protest. "I have your orb, and will not hesitate to destroy it." He was counting on his theory that she needed the crystal to focus and direct her powers.

"It matters not." He felt certain her indifference was feigned. "I have already won, you fool. I no longer need my assistant!" Her eyes were fixed on his hand, and her expression looked thoughtful. *She is weighing her options, and I must act fast.*

"You're lying, witch. You need your globe. Without it, you and I both know that you're an empty and powerless shell."

Sif's face dropped slightly, but quickly recovered her composure. She took a step forward.

"Stop," Rhian ordered, raising the globe higher and slightly behind him, in a gesture that implied that he was prepared to throw it. "I'll send it over the edge, and it will be lost forever!"

She stopped dead in her tracks, holding up both hands, palms out, in grudging conciliation. Her voice had softened. "I love you, Rhian. You and I can start again, now that the barriers to our happiness together have been removed."

Barriers? Sif's plural word choice pointed to an unavoidable and heart-wrenching conclusion. "What have you done with Gwyneth?"

"Ah, Gwyneth," Sif mused, her words steeped in sarcasm. "I tried to call out a warning, but she wouldn't listen. It seems she was unaware of the steep drop on the far side of the stone railing. What a pity, really."

Oh my God. What will I do without Gwyneth? He dropped to his knees again, and a sheet of tears ran down both of his cheeks. "Murderer," he managed to whisper, his voice choked with emotion. "You murdered them *both*!"

She shook her head. "I had nothing to do with either unfortunate accident. The child was taken by your very own kind and loving God when she rolled, on her own accord, off the railing; and your lover simply jumped. It was more like suicide on both accounts, if you ask me." Sif, unaware of the mounting rage in Rhian's warrior's heart, continued

214

her abusive ranting. "Maybe she thought she could save the child, somehow. What a brave and fearless nursemaid. Too bad she sacrificed herself needlessly."

Rhian had heard quite enough, and he stood back up with defiance in his soul. All of the goodness and purity of his spirit surged into his right arm, instantly neutralizing the pain and hatred that emanated from the pulsing orb; and drawing on the whiteness of his inner strength, he stood up and drew his arm back, preparing for the ultimate test of his bravery and integrity. "You will be judged, demon-not by me, but by a higher power! I intend to leave you untouched, but your orb I will destroy!" His intention clear, Rhian cocked back his arm, his powerful muscles tensed like a loaded slingshot as his arm shot forward, aiming high and propelling the globe on a trajectory that would easily clear the railing, with yards to spare, high above Sif's head. He never dreamed that Sif would attempt (or ever be able to) intercept the speeding orb.

The next five seconds seemed to pass in slow motion. Sif reached for the soaring crystal with outstretched arms, as if the gesture would redirect the wayward projectile and alter its course... which it did. Eyes closed in concentration, her lips recited an unnatural incantation; and in direct response, the orb altered its upward trajectory to sharply downward, heading directly for its owner like a perfectly aimed arrow. With horror and dismay, Rhian realized that Sif's summons had succeeded.

But what does the globe intend? It careened towards its mistress at lightning speed, in a path that seemed overtly destructive. Had the orb's contact with Rhian confused its identity? Rhian's hope for a reversal of fortune increased with each passing millisecond, as the globe continued its single-minded dive towards its unsuspecting target. Sif, in the meantime, seemed oblivious to the impending disaster. Eyes closed, she continued to recite her retrieval spell, evidently expecting to reclaim a pliant servant rather than a defiant opponent. The crystal, which was now a fiery red meteor, hurled through the air with whistling precision; and Rhian, anticipating the collision, threw himself face down on the balcony stone. Covering his head with his arms, he watched as the witch's boomerang returned with vengeance to its rightful owner; watched as Sif opened her eyes, just in time to recognize the danger; and watched as she ducked, successfully avoiding direct impact as the vehicle of destruction crashed into the stone railing directly behind her-but there was no explosion and no shattering of the rocky battlement. Instead, the segment of granite that had sustained the impact took in the energy, glowing a fiery red for an instant before it disappeared silently into nothingness, leaving an empty void in place of the solid wall.

But it was far from over. A split second later, Rhian felt an implosion that transformed the six-foot gap into a short-lived vortex, violently sucking the air from the balcony into it and out the other side, leading to the emptiness of the surrounding altitude next to the edge of the tower. Rhian reacted quickly, grabbing onto a metal chain secured to the outside of the central tower wall just in time to prevent him from following Sif through the defect in the balcony railing. He felt his body being lifted and pulled by the orb's violent dissipation, his arms stretched full length while his fingers cramped around the large metal loop, looking back under his levitated body to witness Sif being dragged by a malfunction of her very own body's energy into the empty air beyond, arms flailing as she plummeted out of sight, down to a rocky death far below. A moment later, corresponding it seemed to Sif's final scream when she reached the fateful impact, the supernatural wind abruptly ceased; so Rhian released his life-saving grip and stood on wobbly legs, moving cautiously to an intact segment of wall a safe distance away from the yawning gap, peering fearfully over the edge to confirm that his demon-wife was actually dead-and sure enough there she was, the dark outline of her limp and lifeless body sprawled on the rocks like a discarded and tattered rag doll, lying face down in an expanding pool of blood which washed away as a gentle wave rolled softly over her corpse. *Sif will not rise in this world. Surely, she will rest in hell now, and for all eternity.*

But what about Gwyneth and the baby? He scanned the beach directly below with sadness swelling in his heart; but seeing no sign of them, he concluded that they must have fallen someplace distant, drifting in the wind perhaps (which had started to gust anew) and landing elsewhere, as a result, onto a different rocky location entirely. He leaned over, searching visually to the right, finding nothing; but to the left...

***

217

Gwyneth had realized that she had to act fast if she wished to avert a fatal disaster. She had relied entirely on the accuracy of her prescient nightmare, which had shown her an exterior ledge on the far side of the tower's edge, so as she threw her legs over the battlement she repositioned her hands, gripping the inner edge of the stone railing with desperate fingers. Her arms broke the momentum of her swinging body with a jolt, causing her to ricochet inward as the direction of her velocity became redirected with abrupt and reciprocal intensity. Her torso slammed against the exterior wall and her naked skin slid against the gritty stone, causing her to grit her teeth in reaction to the painful abrasions that she immediately sustained on her breasts, stomach and thighs upon contact. She looked down, thankful that her dream-vision had been accurate, releasing her grip on the edge of the wall and dropping gratefully onto the narrow stone shelf below.

She had been spared the long drop to the rocks below, at least so far; but now the wind started to gust again, blowing forcefully against her and threatening to finish the job that her initial jump had not accomplished. She pressed her nudity flat against the cold stone with a cringing shiver, searching the flat granite with her hands for a defect into which she might insert her aching fingers, finally finding a weathered crack between two frozen stone blocks that nature had widened just enough to accommodate the slim digits of both her hands. *This will do, at least until the wind dies down. Then I will crouch and travel on hands and knees to some safer location.*

218

But what had become of Aibhilin? Gwyneth had hoped to find her on the ledge, in defiance of gravity's persistence that she drop further; and after all, this was the one and only reason that Gwyneth had followed the baby over the edge with such unthinking recklessness. She wasn't here; so how about further to the left? Nothing. Facing the wall again, she waited for a strong gust of wind to pass before looking to the right; because after all, the wind direction would favor a drift that way rather than the other, and the lightness of the baby's body would have allowed such an occurrence. *Please God, let it be so*; and as she glanced apprehensively over her right shoulder, Gwyneth discovered that her silent prayer had been answered.

The helpless infant had fallen, by God's grace, diagonally into a large osprey nest, which was fortuitously situated on the drainage ledge in a perfect position to receive the baby as she fell, pushed over by the strong breeze into the exact center of the bowl-shaped receptacle of entwined twigs, branches and reeds. There she was, resting comfortably on her back without a care in the world, uninjured and safe in a make-shift cradle that had been expertly woven by the very same bird of prey that was majestically perched on the down-sloping tower outcropping, a mere three feet away-the same bird, in fact, that Gwyneth had just recently seen in her dream. Immediately, she got on all fours despite the danger with the wind whipping forcefully against her until she finally reached her destination, whereupon the osprey spread her six-foot wings in an unofficial changing of the guard and left Gwyneth to tend to her charge..

She crouched next to the nest with her right hand on Aibhilin's chest to assure the baby's safety, while the fingers of her left hand found solid purchase on the rim of the osprey nest. There were voices on the balcony, but she could not make out the words. *Is it Rhian? Oh, dear God, if it be him, protect his body and soul from her evil vengeance!* As if in direct answer to her prayer, the adjacent stone railing abruptly disintegrated into thin air just six feet from where Gwyneth knelt on the tower's shelf-like precipice; and a split-second later, a sucking sound was accompanied by someone's blood-curdling scream, apparently coming from a body flying passed, propelled into the dizzying void by what seemed like the devil himself. It was Sif-her burnt copper hair flaming in wild disarray around her beautiful face like Hell-fire itself, her arms flailing against empty air as she dropped like a stone to the rocks below. Gwyneth closed her eyes, thankful that it was the witch rather than Rhian who had been thrown by some twisted magic off the battlement tower to meet her death.

"It's over," she declared, which Rhian confirmed a moment later when he reached for her over the edge of eternity with the howling winter wind blowing around them. Their eyes locked, and at that moment she knew, without a doubt, that their new life together had just begun.

Chapter 9
In the castle's banquet hall

As told by Caetie
Ten years later

After the witch's demise, Rhian took the beautiful Gwyneth as his wife and lady; and never before, or after, would there be a more perfect union between a man and a woman. Gwyneth's sister, Caetie, never found her son's father, and she could not bring herself to give her heart to another. A single mother, she moved into the castle with her son, Seoc; and although a passing minstrel had sired the boy, Rhian raised Seoc as his own beloved son, along with Aibhilin and yet another daughter, Daera, born the next summer as the result of Rhian and Gwyneth's unbridled passion.

The year was now 1153. Olaf was dead; and Somerled, the Regent of Kinn Tyre, was gathering allies in his fastidious plan to claim the throne of Mann. Somerled's wife, Olaf's daughter Raghnailt, had recently died of pleurisy. Had she lived, the Hebrides may well have been handed to Somerled, as the dead king's son-in-law, uncontested; but as things stood, Olaf's brother-in-law, Goraidh, had declared himself king, and Somerled would have to fight for his view of the less-than-certain line of succession. The powerful warlord was now recruiting followers, as well as looking for a new wife. Not only was Somerled dashing and handsome, but the general consensus predicted that he would easily prevail against Goraidh in the struggle for the throne, making him a most desirable potential husband for all of the kingdom's eligible maidens.

It was the day of Somerled's visit to Dunyvaig to assure Rhian's allegiance, ten years almost to the day after Gwyneth had become Rhian's wife and the Lady of Islay. Caetie had just seated herself next to her sister at the front table in the castle's enormous banquet hall, waiting for the welcoming party's imminent arrival.

"They say the Regent searches for a queen," Gwyneth nonchalantly said. "Perhaps he will choose you."

"I cannot forget my minstrel. If I am destined to be alone as my punishment for loving him completely, then so be it."

"We are so alike, you and I, so I truly cannot blame you. I sacrificed everything to pursue my one true love, so why shouldn't you?"

She shrugged. "At least I have my Seoc as a reminder."

"If he looks as his father does when he ages into manhood, perhaps the one will recognize the other in some chance meeting, and thus cause your small family to reunite."

"Perhaps. What think you, Gwyneth, of this future king?"

"I have never met him. They say he is charming, strong and handsome; but we shall see momentarily for ourselves, shan't we?"

As if on command, the doors swung open to admit the Thane of Islay and his influential guest, Somerled, the future King of Mann and the Isles.

222

Caetie immediately pushed back her chair in haste, the moment she saw Rhian's companion.

"Caetie!" Gwyneth called after her. "Where in the world are you going?"

She didn't answer, but instead rushed from the table and down the three or four stairs that led from the raised platform to the hall proper, gathering her skirts as she ran as fast as she could on the unrolled welcome-carpet towards her brother-in-law and his notable guest. Rhian had barely stammered the first word or two of an awkward introduction (in retrospect quite unnecessary) before Caetie literally threw herself into the stranger's arms. "You have returned," she sobbed between kisses.

"I have indeed, my darling," Somerled answered. "I knew exactly where to find you."

Caetie's minstrel had finally returned.

THE END